Henry Headley

Select Beauties of Ancient English Poetry

With remarks. Vol. 2

Henry Headley

Select Beauties of Ancient English Poetry
With remarks. Vol. 2

ISBN/EAN: 9783337105587

Printed in Europe, USA, Canada, Australia, Japan

Cover: Foto ©Andreas Hilbeck / pixelio.de

More available books at **www.hansebooks.com**

SELECT BEAUTIES

OF

ANCIENT ENGLISH POETRY.

WITH REMARKS

By HENRY HEADLEY, A. B.

THE MONUMENT OF BANISH'D MINDES.

Sr W. Davenant

NON OMNIS
MORIAR.

LONDON,

Printed for T. CADELL, in the Strand.

MDCCLXXXVII.

(v)

CONTENTS

OF

VOLUME the SECOND.

DIDACTIC and MORAL PIECES.

ELEGIES and EPITAPHS.

MISCEL-

⟨ MISCELLANEOUS PIECES.

S O N N E T S.

S P E E C H E S.

DIDACTIC

DIDACTIC AND MORAL PIECES.

My MIDNIGHT MEDITATION.

ILL-bufi'd Man! why fhould'ft thou take fuch care
To lengthen out thy life's fhort Kalendar?
When ev'ry fpectacle thou look'ft upon
Prefents and acts thy execution.
 Each drooping feafon and each flower doth cry,
 " Fool! as I fade and wither, thou muft dy."

The beating of thy pulfe (when thou art well)
Is juft the tolling of thy paffing bell :
Night is thy hearfe, whofe fable canopie
Covers alike deceafed day and thee.
 And all thofe weeping dewes which nightly fall,
 Are but the tears fhed for thy funerall.
Dr. King's Poems, p. 138.

TIMES GOE BY TURNES.

THE lopped tree in time may grow againe,
   Moſt naked plants renew both fruite and flower:
The ſorrieſt wight may find releaſe of paine,
The dryeſt ſoyle ſucke in ſome moyſtning ſhower,
Times goe by turnes, and chaunces change by courſe,
From foule to faire: from better hap to worſe.

The ſea of Fortune doth not ever flow,
Shee drawes her favours to the loweſt ebbe;
Her tides have equall times to come and goe,
Her loome doth weave the fine and courſeſt webbe.
No joy ſo great, but runneth to an end:
No hap ſo hard, but may in fine amend.

Not alwaies fall of leafe, nor ever ſpring,
No endleſſe night, nor yet eternall day;
The ſaddeſt birds a ſeaſon find to ſing,
The rougheſt ſtorme a calme may ſoon allay.
Thus with ſucceeding turnes God tempereth all:
That man may hope to riſe, yet feare to fall.

A chaunce

A chaunce may winne that by mifchaunce was loft,
That net that holds no great, takes little fifh ;
In fome things all, in all things none are croft,
Fewe all they need, but none have all they wifh:
Unmeddled joyes here to no man befall:
Who leaft, hath fome, who moft, hath never all.

Robert Southwell.

The SEARCH after FELICITY.

THE wifeft men, that Nature e're could boaft,
 For fecret knowledge of her power, were loft,
Confounded, and in deepe amazement ftood,
In the difcovery of the Chiefeft Good :
Keenly they hunted, beat in every bracke,
Forwards they went, on either hand, and backe
Return'd they counter ; but their deep-mouth'd art
(Though often challeng'd fent) yet ne're could ftart
In all th' enclofures of Philofophy,
That game, from fquat, they terme, Felicity:
They jangle, and their maxims difagree,
As many men, fo many mindes there be:
 One digs to Pluto's throne, thinks there to finde
Her Grace, rak't up in gold : another's minde
Mounts to the Courts of Kings, with plumes of honor
And feather'd hopes, hopes there to feize upon her ;
A third, unlockes the painted gates of Pleafure,
And ranfacks there, to find this peerleffe treafure,
A fourth, more fage, more wifely melancholy,
Perfwades himfelfe, her Deity's too holy

B 2

For

For common hands to touch, he rather chufes,
To make a long dayes journey to the Mufes :
To Athens (gown'd) he goes, and from that Schoole
Returnes unfped, a more inftructed foole.
    Where lyes fhe then ? or lyes fhe any where ?
Honours are bought and fold, fhe refts not there,
Much leffe in Pleafures hath fhe her abiding,
For they are fhar'd to Beafts, and ever fliding ;
Nor yet in Vertue, Vertue's often poore ;
And (crufh't with fortune) begs from doore to door,
Nor is fhe fainted in the fhrine of Wealth ;
That, makes men flaves, is unfecur'd from ftealth ;
Conclude we then, Felicity confifts
Not in exteriour fortunes, but her lifts
Are boundleffe, and her large extenfion
Out-runnes the pafe of humane apprehenfion ;
Fortunes are feldome meafur'd by defert,
The fairer face, hath oft the fouler heart ;
Sacred Felicity doth ne'er extend
Beyond itfelfe ; in it, all wifhes end :
The fwelling of an outward fortune can
Create a profp'rous, not a happy man ;
A peacefull Confcience is the true Content,
And Wealth is but her golden ornament.

                              Job Militant,
                              13 Med. by F. Quarlés.
                              Edit 1630. Lond.

.

                                        SCORN

SCORN NOT THE LEAST.

WHERE wards are weak, and foes encountring ſtrong,
Where mightier do aſſault then doe defend,
The feebler part puts up enforced wrong,
And ſilent ſees that ſpeech could not amend ;
Yet higher powers muſt thinke, though they repine,
When ſunne is ſet, the little ſtarres will ſhine.

While pike do range, the ſilly tench doth flie,
And crouch in privie creekes, with ſmaller fiſh :
Yet pikes are caught when little fiſh goe by,
Theſe fleete aflote, while thoſe doe fill the diſh ;
There is a time even for the wormes to creepe,
And ſucke the deaw while all their foes doe ſleepe.

The marline cannot ever ſoare on high,
Nor greedie grey-hound ſtill purſue the chaſe,
The tender larke will finde a time to flie,
And fearfull hare to runne a quiet race.
He that high growth on cedars did beſtow,
Gave alſo lowly muſhrumps leave to growe.

In

In Haman's pompe poor Mordocheus wept;
Yet God did turne his fate upon his foe.
The Lazar pinde, while Dives feaſt was kept,
Yet he to Heaven, to Hell did Dives goe.
We trample graſſe, and prize the flowers of May,
Yet graſſe is greene, when flowers doe fade away.

Robert Southwell.

The Diſtinction between WISDOM and KNOWLEDGE.

THE Morall Poets, (nor unaptly) faine
    That by lame Vulcans help, the pregnant brain
Of ſoveraigne Jove, brought forth, and at that birth,
Was borne Minerva, Lady of the earth.
    O ſtrange Divinity! but ſung by rote;
Sweet is the tune, but in a wilder note.
The morall ſayes, all wiſedome that is given
To hood-wink't mortals, firſt, proceeds from heaven
Truth's errour, Wiſedome's but wiſe inſolence,
And light's but darkneſſe, not deriv'd from thence;
Wiſdom's a ſtraine tranſcends Morality,
No vertue's abſent, Wiſedome being by.
Vertue, by conſtant practice is acquir'd,
This (this by ſweat unpurchaſt) is inſpir'd:
The maſter-piece of knowledge, is to know
But what is good, from what is good in ſhow,
And there it reſts: Wiſdome proceeds, and chuſes
The ſeeming evill, th' apparent good refuſes;

Knowledge

Knowledge defcries alone ; Wifdome applyes,
That, makes fome fooles, this, maketh none but wife ;
The curious hand of Knowledge doth but picke
Bare fimples, Wifdome pounds them, for the ficke ;
In my afflictions, Knowledge apprehends,
Who is the author, what the caufe and ends,
It findes that Patience is my fad reliefe,
And that the hand that caus'd, can cure my griefe :
To reft contented here, is but to bring
Clouds without raine, and heat without a fpring :
What hope arifes hence ? the devils doe
The very fame : they know and tremble too ;
But facred Wifedome doth apply that good,
Which fimple knowledge barely underftood :
Wifedome concludes, and in conclufion, proves
That wherefoever God correct, he loves :
Wifedome digefts, what Knowledge did but taft,
That deales in futures, this, in things are paft :
Wifdom's the card of Knowledge, which, without
That guide, at random's wreck't on every doubt :
Knowledge, when Wifdome is too weak to guide her
Is like a head-ftrong horfe, that throwes the rider :
Which made that great Philofopher avow,
He knew fo much that he did nothing know.

Job. Militant, Med. II. Edit. 1630.
by F. Quarles.

The

The Infufficiency of monumental honours to preferve the Memory.

YOU mighty Lords, that with refpected grace
   Do at the ftern of fair example ftand,
And all the body of this populace
Guide with the turning of your hand ;
Keep a right courfe; bear up from all difgrace ;
Obferve the point of glory to our Land:

Hold up difgraced Knowledge from the ground ;
Keep Virtue in requeft ; give Worth her due.
Let not Neglect with barb'rous means confound
So fair a good, to bring in Night a-new :
Be not, O be not acceffary found
Unto her death, that muft give life to you.

Where will you have your virtuous name fafe laid
In gorgeous tombs, in facred cells fecure ?
Do you not fee thofe proftrate heaps betray'd
Your Father's bones, and could not keep them fure ?
And will you truft deceitful ftones fair laid,
And think they will be to your honour truer ?

No, no; unfparing Time will proudly fend
A warrant unto Wrath, that with one frown
Will all thefe mockries of vain-glory rend,
And make them (as before) ungrac'd, unknown ;
Poor idle honours, that can ill defend
Your memories, that cannot keep their own.

And

And whereto ſerve that wondrous Trophee now
That on the goodly plain near Walton ſtands?
That huge dumb heap, that cannot tell us how,
Nor what, nor whence it is; nor with whoſe hands,
Nor for whoſe glory—it was ſet to ſhew,
How much our pride mocks that of other Lands.

Whereon when as the gazing Paſſenger
Hath greedy look'd with admiration;
And fain would know his birth, and what he were;
How there erected; and how long agon:
Enquires and aſks his fellow traveller
What he hath heard, and his opinion:

And he knows nothing, then he turns again,
And looks and ſighs; and then admires afreſh,
And in himſelf with ſorrow doth complain
The miſery of dark forgetfulneſs:
Angry with Time that nothing ſhould remain,
Our greateſt Wonders Wonder to expreſs.

Then Ignorance, with fabulous diſcourſe,
Robbing fair Art and Cunning of their right,
Tells how thoſe ſtones were by the Devil's force
From Afric brought to Ireland in a night;
And thence to Britany, by magick courſe,
From Giant's hands redeem'd by Merlin's ſlight;

And then near Ambri plac'd in memory
Of all thoſe noble Britons murther'd there,
By Hengiſt and his Saxon treachery,
Coming to parlee in peace at unaware,
With this old legend then Credulity
Holds her content, and cloſes up her care.

And

* And as for thee, thou huge and mighty frame,
That ſtands corrupted ſo with Time's deſpite,
And giv'lt falſe evidence againſt their fame
That ſet thee there to teſtify their right ;
And are become a traitor to their name,
That truſted thee with all the beſt they might;

Thou ſhalt ſtand ſtill bely'd and ſlandered,
The only gazing-ſtock of Ignorance,
And by thy guile the wiſe admoniſhed,
Shall never more deſire ſuch hopes t' advance,
Nor truſt their living glory with the dead
That cannot ſpeak, but leave their fame to chance.

Conſid'ring in how ſmall a room do lie,
And yet lie ſafe, (as freſh as if alive)
All thoſe great Worthies of Antiquity,
Which long foreliv'd thee, and ſhall long ſurvive ;
Who ſtronger tombs found for Eternity,
Than could the Pow'rs of all the Earth contrive.

Where they remain theſe trifles to upbraid,
Out of the reach of ſpoil, and way of Rage;
Tho' Time with all his Pow'r of years hath laid
Long batt'ry, back'd with undermining Age ;
Yet they make head only with their own aid,
And war with his all-conqu'ring forces wage;
Pleading the Heavens preſcription to be free,
And t' have a grant t' endure as long as He.

Muſophilus. by S. Daniel.

* A few lines of inferior merit are here omitted.

THE

The IDEA BEATIFICAL,

* * * * * * * * * * *
'End, and Beginning of each thing that growes,
Whofe felfe no end, nor yet beginning knowes,
 That hath no eyes to fee, nor ears to heare,
 Yet fees and heares, and is all eye, all eare,
That no whear is contain'd, and yet is every whear.

Changer of all things, yet immutable,
Before and after all, the firft, and laft,
That mooving all, is yet immoveable,
Great without quantitie, in whofe forecaft,
Things paft are prefent, things to come are paft ;
 Swift without motion, to whofe open eye,
 The hearts of wicked men unbretted lie,
At once abfent, and prefent to them, farre and nigh.

It is no flaming luftre, made of light,
No fweet concent, or well-tim'd harmonie,
Ambrofia, for to feaft the appetite,
Or flowrie odour mixt with fpicerie.
No foft embrace, or pleafure bodilily,
 And yet it is a kind of inward feaft,
 A harmony, that founds within the breaft,
An odour, light, embrace, in which the foule doth reft.

       A heav'nly

A heav'nly feaſt, no hunger can confume,
A light unſeene, yet ſhines in every place,
A ſound, no time can ſteale, a ſweet perfume
No windes can ſcatter, an entire embrace,
That no ſatietie can ere unlace,
  Ingrac't into ſo high a favour, thear
  The Saints, with their beaw-peers, whole worlds outwear,
And things unſeene doe ſee, and things unheard doe hear.

       Chriſt's Triumph,
       Part II. Stan. 38—41.
       Ed. 1610. by G. Fletcher.

REFLECTIONS on DEATH,

TH' Egyptians, amidſt their ſolemne feaſts,
 Uſed to welcome, and preſent their gueſts
With the ſad ſight of Man's anatomy,
Serv'd in with this loud motto, " *All muſt die.*"
Fooles often goe about, when as they may
Take better vantage of a neerer way.
Looke well into your boſomes: doe not flatter
Your knowne infirmities: behold, what matter
Your fleſhe was made of: Man, caſt backe thine eye,
Upon the weakneſſe of thine infancy;
See how thy lips hang on thy mother's breſt
Bawling for helpe, more helpleſſe than a beaſt.
 Liv'ſt thou to Childhood? then, behold, what toies
Doe mocke the ſenſe, how ſhallow are thy joyes.

           Com'ſt

Com'ft thou to downie yeares ? See, how deceits
Gull thee with golden fruit, and with falfe baits
Slily beguile the prime of thine affection.
Art thou attain'd at length to full perfection
Of ripen'd yeares ? Ambition hath now fent
Thee on her frothy errand ; Difcontent
Payes thee thy wages. Doe thy grizly haires
Begin to caft account of many cares
Upon thy head ? The facred luft of gold
Now fires thy fpirit, for flefhly luft too cold,
Makes thee a flave to thine owne bafe defire,
Which melts and hardens at the felf fame fire.
Art thou decrepit ? then thy very breath
Is grievous to thee, and each griefe's a death.
Looke where thou lift, thy life is but a fpan,
Thou art but duft, and, to conclude, a Man.
Thy life's a warfare, thou a fouldier art,
Satan's thy foe-man, and a faithfull heart
Thy two-edg'd weapon, patience thy fhield,
Heaven is thy Chiefetain, and the world thy field.
To be afraid to die, or wifh for death,
Are words and paffions of defpairing breath :
Who doth the firft, the day doth faintly yeeld,
And who the fecond, bafely flies the field.
Man's not a lawfull ftearfman of his dayes,
His bootleffe wifh, nor haftens nor delayes :
We are God's hired workmen ; he difcharges
Some late at night, and (when he lift) inlarges
Others at noone, and in the morning, fome :
None may relieve himfelfe, till he bid come :
If we receive for one halfe day as much
As they that toyle till evening, fhall we grutch ?

Job Militant,
Med. 8. by F. Quarles.
Ed. 1630.

The

The Immortality of the SOUL, implied from its Motion.

————The Soul, which in this earthly mould
The fpirit of God doth fecretly infufe,
Becaufe at firft fhe doth th' Earth behold,
And only this material world fhe views :

At firft her mother Earth fhe holdeth dear,
And doth embrace the world, and worldly things ;
She flies clofe by the ground, and hovers here,
And mounts not up with her celeftial wings.

Yet under heav'n fhe cannot light on aught
That with her heavenly nature doth agree ;
She cannot reft, fhe cannot fix her thought,
She cannot in this world contented be.

For who did ever yet, in Honour, Wealth,
Or Pleafure of the fence, contentment find ?
Who ever ceas'd to wifh when he had Health ?
Or having Wifdom was not vext in mind ?

With this defire fhe hath a native might
To find out every truth if fhe had time ;
Th' innumerable effects to fort aright,
And by degree from caufe to caufe to climb.

But

But fince our life fo faft away doth flide,
As doth a hungry Eagle through the wind:
Or as a fhip tranfported with the tide,
Which in their paffage leave no print behind;

Of which fwift little time fo much we fpend
While fome few things we through the fence do ftrain,
That our fhort race of life is at an end,
Ere we the principles óf fkill attain.

Sir John Davies,
p. 68.

The Inftability of HUMAN GREATNESS.

FOND Man, that looks on Earth for happineffe,
  And here long feeks what here is never found!
For all our good we hold from heav'n by leafe,
With many forfeits and conditions bound;
    Nor can we pay the fine and rentage due;
    'Though now but writ, and feal'd, and giv'n anew,
  Yet daily we it break, then daily mult renew.

Why fhould'ft thou here look for perpetuall good,
A every loffe againft heav'ns face repining?
Do but behold where glorious Cities ftood,
With gilded tops, and filver turrets fhining;
    There now the Hart fearleffe of grey-hound feeds,
    And loving Pelican in fafety breeds;
  There fhrieching Satyres fill the people's emptie fteads.

7   Where

Where is th' Affyrian Lion's golden hide,
That all the Eaſt once graſpt in lordly paw?
Where that great Perſian Peare, whoſe ſwelling pride
The Lion's ſelf tore out with ravenous jaw?
 Or he which twixt a Lion and a Pard,
 Through all the World with nimble pineons far'd,
And to his greedy whelps his conquer'd kingdomes ſhar'd?

Hardly the place of ſuch antiquitie,
Or note of theſe great monarchies we finde:
Onely a fading verball memorie,
And empty name in writ is left behinde:
 But when this ſecond life, and glory fades,
 And ſinks at length in times obſcurer ſhades,
A ſecond fall ſucceeds, and double death invades.

That monſtrous beaſt, which nurſt in Tiber's ferne
Did all the world with hideous ſhape affray;
That fill'd with coſtly ſpoil his gaping denne,
And trode downe all the reſt to duſt and clay:
 His batt'ring horns, pull'd out by civil hands,
 And iron teeth, lie ſcatter'd on the ſands;
Back't, bridled by a Monk with ſeven heads yoked ſtands.

And that black Vulture, which with deathfull wing
Ore-ſhadowes half the Earth, whoſe diſmal ſight
Frighted the Muſes from their native ſpring,
Already ſtoops, and flagges with weary flight.
 Who then ſhall hope for happines beneath;
 Where each new day proclaims chance, change and death,
And life itſelf's as flit as is the aire we breathe?

Purple Iſland,
Cant. 7, St. 2—7;
by Ph. Fletcher. Edit. 1633.

FAITH.

FAITH.

THE proudeſt pitch of that victorious Spirit
　Was but to win the World, whereby t' inherite
The ayrie purchaſe of a tranſitory
And glozing title of an age's glory ;
Would'ſt thou by conqueſt win more fame than he,
Subdue thyſelfe ; thyſelfe's a world to thee.
Earth's but a ball, that Heaven hath quilted ore
With Wealth and Honour, banded on the floore
Of fickle Fortune's falſe and ſlippery Court,
Sent for a Toy, to make us Children ſport,
Man's ſatiate ſpirits with freſh delights ſupplying,
To ſtill the fondlings of the world from crying ;
And he, whoſe merit mounts to ſuch a joy,
Gaines but the honour of a mighty toy.
　But would'ſt thou conquer, have thy conqueſt crown'd
By hands of Seraphims, trymph'd with the ſound
Of Heaven's loud trumpet, warbled by the ſhrill
Celeſtial quire, recorded with a quill,
Pluckt from the pinion of an Angels wing,
Confirm'd with joy by Heavens eternal King ;
Conquer thyſelfe, thy rebel thoughts repell,
And chaſe thoſe falſe affections that rebell.
Hath Heaven deſpoil'd what his full hand hath given thee ?
Nipt thy ſucceeding bloſſomes ? or bereaven thee,
Of thy deare lateſt hope, thy boſome friend ?
Doth ſad Deſpaire deny theſe griefes an end ?
Deſpaire's a whiſp'ring rebell, that within thee,
Bribes all thy field, and ſets thy ſelfe agin thee :

VOL. II. 　　　　　C 　　　　　　　Make

Make keene thy faith, and with thy force let flee,
If thou not conquer him, he'll conquer thee :
Advance thy fhield of Patience to thy head,
And when Griefe ftriks, 'twil ftrike the ftriker dead.
* In adverfe fortunes, be thou ftrong and ftout,
And bravely win thyfelfe, Heaven holds not out
His bow for ever bent ; the difpofition
Of nobleft fpirit, doth, by oppofition,
Exafperate the more : a gloomy night
Whets on the morning to returne more bright ;
† Brave minds, oppreft, fhould in defpight of Fate,
Looke greateft, like the Sune, in loweft ftate.
But, ah ! fhall God thus ftrive with flefh and blood ?
Receives he glory from, or reapes he good
In mortals ruine, that he leaves man fo
To be overwhelm'd by this unequall foe ?
  May not a Potter, that, from out the ground,
Hath fram'd a veffel, fearch if it be found ?
Or if, by furbifhing, he take more paine
To make it fairer, fhall the pot complaine ?
Mortall, thou art but clay : then fhall not he,
That fram'd thee for his fervice, feafon thee ?
Man, cloze thy lips ; be thou no undertaker
Of God's defignes ; difpute not with thy Maker.

                              Job Mil. 3 Med.
                              Ed. 1638, by F. Quarles.

---

* Two lines are here omitted.
† Two lines are here omitted.

To the Honourable Mr. W. E——.

HE who is good is happy—let the loude
    Artillery of Heaven breake through a cloude,
And dart its thunder at him ; hee'le remaine
Unmov'd and nobler comfort entertaine
In welcomming th' approach of Death, then Vice,
Ere found in her fictitious Paradife.
Time mocks our youth, and (while we number paft
Delights, and raife our appetite to tafte
Enfuing) brings us to unflatter'd Age,
Where we are left to fatisfie the rage
Of threatning Death : Pompe, Beauty, Wealth, and all
Our Friendfhips, fhrinking from the funerall.
The thought of this begets that brave difdaine
With which thou view'ft the world, and makes thofe vaine
Treafures of fancy, ferious fooles fo court,
And fweat to purchafe, thy contempt or fport.
What fhould we covet here ? why interpofe
A cloud twixt us and Heaven ? kind Nature chofe
Man's foule th' Exchequer where fhe'd hoord her wealth,
And lodge all her rich fecrets ; but by the ftealth
Of our owne vanity, w' are left fo poore,
The creature meerely fenfuall knowes more.
The learned Halcyon by her wifdome finds
A gentle feafon, when the feas and winds
Are filenc't by a calme, and then brings forth
The happy miracle of her rare birth,
Leaving with wonder all our arts poffeft,
That view the architecture of her neft.

Pride

Pride raiſeth us 'bove juſtice.   We beſtowe
Increaſe of knowledge on old minds, which grow
By age to dotage ; while the ſenſitive
Part of the world in its firſt ſtrength doth live.
Folly ! what doſt thou in thy power containe
Deſerves our ſtudy ? merchants plough the maine,
And bring home th' Indies, yet aſpire to more,
By avarice in the poſſeſſion poore.
And yet that Idol Wealth we all admite
Into the ſoule's great Temple, buſie Wit
Invents new orgies, Fancy frames new rites
To ſhew its ſuperſtition, anxious nights
Are watcht to win its favour ; while the beaſt
Content with Nature's courteſie doth reſt.
Let man then boaſt no more a ſoule, ſince he
Hath loſt that great prerogative ; but thee
(Whom Fortune hath exempted from the herd
Of vulgar men, whom Vertue hath preferr'd
Farre higher than thy birth) I muſt commend,
Rich in the purchaſe of ſo ſweete a friend.
And though my fate conducts me to the ſhade
Of humble Quiet, my ambition payde
With ſafe content, while a pure Virgin fame
Doth raiſe me trophies in Caſtara's name.
No thought of glory ſwelling me above
The hope of being famed for vertuous love.
Yet wiſh I thee, guided by better ſtarres
To purchaſe unſafe honour in the warres
Or envied ſmiles at Court ; for thy great race,
And merits well may challenge th' higheſt place.
Yet know, what buſie path ſo-ere you tread
To Greatneſſe, you muſt ſleepe among the dead.

Caſtara, by W. Habington,
Ed, Lond, 1640.

SIC

SIC VITA.

LIKE to the falling of a ftarre;
Or as the flights of Eagles are;
Or like the frefh Spring's gaudy hew:
Or filver drops of morning dew;
Or like a wind that chafes the flood;
Or bubbles which on water ftood;
Even fuch is Man, whofe borrow'd light
Is ftreight call'd in, and paid to night.

The Wind blowes out; the Bubble dies;
The Spring entomb'd in Autumn lies;
The Dew dries up; the Starre is fhot:
The flight is paft; and Man forgot.

Dr. King's Poems,
page 139.

To

To my nobleft Friend J. C———, Efquire,

S I R,

I Hate the Countries durt and manners, yet
I love the filence ; I embrace the wit
And courtfhip, flowing here in a full tide,
But loathe the expence, the vanity and pride.
No place each way is happy ; here I hold
Commerce with fome, who to my eare unfold
(After a due oath miniftred) the height
And greatnelle of each ftar fhines in the ftate,
The brightnelle, the eclypfe, the influence.
With others I commune, who tell me whence
The torrent doth of forraigne difcord flow :
Relate each fkirmifh, battle, overthrow,
Soon as they happen ; and by rote can tell
Thofe Germane townes, even puzzle me to fpell,
The croffe or profperous fate of Princes, they
Afcribe to rafhneffe, cunning, or delay :
And on each action comment with more fkill
Then upon Livy, did old Matchavill.
O bufie folly ! why doe I my braine
Perplex with the dull pollicies of Spaine,
Or quicke defignes of France ? why not repaire
To the pure innocence of the Country ayre.
And neighbor thee, deare friend ? who fo doft give
Thy thoughts to worth and vertue, that to live
Bleft, is to trace thy wayes, there, might not we
Arme againft Paffion with Philofophie ;

5   And

And by the aide of leifure, fo controule
Whate'er is earth in us, to grow all foule ?
Knowledge doth ignorance ingender when
We ftudy mifteries of other men
And forraigne plots.   Doe but in thy owne fhade
Thy head upon fome flowry pillow laide,
(Kind Nature's hufwifery) contemplate all
His ftratagems who labours to inthrall
The world to his great Mafter ; and you'le finde
Ambition mockes itfelfe, and grafpes the wind.
Not conqueft makes us great, blood is too deare
A price for Glory : Honour doth appeare
To ftatefmen like a vifion in the night,
And juggler-like workes on the deluded fight.
The unbufied only wife : for no refpect
Indangers them to error ; they affect
Truth in her naked beauty, and behold
Man with an equall eye, not bright in gold
Or tall in title ; fo much him they weigh
As Vertue raifeth him above his clay.
Thus let us value things ; and fince we find
Time bends us toward death, let's in our mind
Create new Youth, and arme againft the rude
Affaults of age ; that no dull folitude
Of the Country dead our thoughts, nor bufie care
Of the towne make us not thinke, where now we are
And whether we are bound ; Time nere forgot
His journey, though his fteps we numbred not.

Caftara, by W. Habington.
Ed, 1640. Lond.

C 4   A Farewell

A Farewell to the Vanities of the World.

FAREWELL, ye gilded follies, pleasing troubles;
Farewell, ye honour'd rags, ye glorious bubbles;
Fame's but a hollow echo, gold pure clay;
Honour the darling but of one short day.
Beauty, th' eye's idol but a damask'd skin;
State but a golden prison to live in,
And torture free-born minds : embroider'd trains
Merely but pageants for proud swelling veins ;
And blood ally'd to greatnefs, is alone
Inherited, not purchas'd nor our own,
   Fame, honour, beauty, state, train, blood and birth,
   Are but the fading blossoms of the earth.

I would be great, but that the sun doth still
Level his rays against the rising hill :
I would be high, but see the proudest oak
Most subject to the rending thunder-stroke :
I would be rich, but see men too unkind,
Dig in the bowels of the richest mind :
I would be wise, but that I often see
The fox suspected, whilst the ass goes free :
I would be fair, but see the fair and proud
Like the bright sun, oft setting in a cloud :
I would be poor, but know the humble grass
Still trampled on by each unworthy ass :
Rich hated : wise suspected : scorn'd if poor :
Great fear'd : fair tempted : high still envy'd more :
   I have wish'd all ; but now I wish for neither ;
   Great, high, rich, wise nor fair ; poor I'll be rather.

                                        Would

Would the World now adopt me for her heir,
Would Beauty's Queen entitle me " The Fair,"
Fame fpeak me Fortune's minion, could I vie
Angels with India ; with a fpeaking eye
Command bare heads, bow'd knees, ftrike Juftice dumb,
As well as blind and lame, or give a tongue
To ftones by epitaphs : be call'd Great Mafter
In the loofe rhimes of every poetafter ?
Could I be more than any man that lives,
Great, fair, rich, wife, all in fuperlatives :
Yet I more freely would thefe gifts refign,
Than ever fortune would have made them mine,
    And hold one minute of this holy leifure,
    Beyond the riches of this empty pleafure.

Welcome pure thoughts, welcome ye filent groves ,
Thefe guefts, thefe courts, my foul moft dearly loves :
Now the wing'd people of the fky fhall fing
My chearful anthems to the gladfome fpring :
A prayer-book now fhall be my looking-glafs,
In which I will adore fweet Virtues face.
Here dwell no hateful looks, no palace-cares,
No broken vows dwell here, nor pale-fac'd fears :
Then here I'll fit, and figh my hot love's folly,
And learn t' affect an holy melancholy ;
    And if Contentment be a ftranger then,
    I'll ne'er look for it, but in Heaven again.
                    Sir H. Wotton.

The

The SHORTNESS of LIFE.

MY glafs is half unfpent ; forbear t' arreft
My thriftlefs day too foon : my poor requeft
Is that my glafs may run but out the reft.

My time-devouring minutes will be done
Without thy help ; fee ! fee how fwift they run :
Cut not my thread before my thread be fpun.

The gaines not great I purchafe by this ftay ;
What lofs fuftain'it thou by fo fmall delay,
To whom ten thoufand years are but a day ?

My following eye can hardly make a fhift
To count my winged hours ; they fly fo fwift,
They fcarce deferve the bounteous name of gift.

The fecret wheels of hurrying time do give
So fhort a warning, and fo faft they drive,
That I am dead before I feem to live.

And what's a life ? a weary pilgrimage,
Whofe glory in one day doth fill the ftage
With Childhood, Manhood, and decrepit Age.

And what's a life ? the flourifhing array
Of the prond fummer-meadow, which to-day
Weares her green plufh, and is to-morrow hay.

Read on this dial, how the fhades devour
My fhort-lived winter's day ! hour eats up hour;
Alas ! the total's but from eight to four.

Behold thefe lilies, which thy hands have made
Fair copies of my life, and open laid
To view, how foon they droop, how foon they fade !

Shade not that dial, night will blind too foon ;
My non-aged day already points to noon ;
How fimple is my fuit I how fmall my boon !

Nor do I beg this flender inch, to wile
The time away, or falfely to beguile
My thoughts with joy ; here's nothing worth a fmile.

Quarles Emblems.

B. 3. Em. 13.

O That

O That thou wouldſt hide me in the Grave, that thou
wouldſt keep me in ſecret until thy wrath be paſt.

PSALMS

AH! whither ſhall I fly? what path untrod
Shall I ſeek out to 'ſcape the flaming rod
Of my offended, of my angry God?

Where ſhall I ſojourn? what kind ſea will hide
My head from thunder? where ſhall I abide,
Until his flames be quench'd or laid aſide?

What if my feet ſhould take their haſty flight,
And ſeek protection in the ſhades of night?
Alas! no ſhades can blind the God of Light.

What if my ſoul ſhould take the wings of day,
And find ſome deſert; if ſhe ſpring away,
The wings of Vengeance clip as faſt as they.

What if ſome ſolid rock ſhould entertain
My frighted ſoul? can ſolid rocks reſtrain
The ſtroke of Juſtice and not cleave in twain?

Nor ſea, nor ſhade, nor ſhield, nor rock, nor cave,
Nor ſilent deſerts, nor the ſullen grave,
Where flame-ey'd fury means to ſmite, can ſave.

'Tis vain to flee; 'till gentle Mercy ſhew
Her better eye; the farther off we go,
The ſwing of Juſtice deals the mightier blow.

Th

Th' ingenuous child, corrected, doth not flie
His angry mother's hand, but clings more nigh,
And quenches with his tears her flaming eye.

Great God! there is no fafety here below;
Thou art my fortrefs, thou that feem'ft my foe,
Tis thou that ftrik'ft the ftroke, muft guard the blow.

Quarles Emblems.

ALL THINGS ARE VAINE.

A LTHOUGH the purple morning, brages in brightnefs of
the funne
As though he had of chafed night, a glorious conqueft
wonne:
The time by day, gives place againe to force of drowfy night,
And every creature is conftrain'd to change his lufty plight.
    Of pleafure all that here we tafte;
    We feele the contrary at lafte.

In fpring, though pleafant Zephirus hath frutefull earth
infpired,
And Nature hath each bufh, each branch, with bloffomes
brave attired:
Yet fruites and flowers, as buds and blomes ful quickly
withered be,
When ftormie Winter comes to kill, the Sommers jollitie.
    By time are got, by time are loft,
    All thinges wherein we pleafure moft.

3

Although

Although the Seas fo calmely glide, as daungers none ap-
 peare,
And dout of ftormes, in fkie is none, king Phœbus fhines fo
 cleare:
Yet when the boiftrous windes breake out, and raging waves
 do fwel,
The feely barke now heaves to heaven, now finkes againe
 to hel,
  Thus change in ever thing we fee,
  And nothing conftant feemes to be.

Who floweth moft in worldly wealth of wealth is moft unfure,
And he that cheefely taftes of joy, doth fometime woe endure:
Who vaunteth moft of numbred freendes, foregoe them all he
 muft,
The faireft flefh and livelieft bloud, is turn'd at length to duft.
  Experience gives a certain ground,
  That certen here, is nothing found.

Then truft to that which aye remaines, the bliffe of heavens
 above,
Which Time, nor Fate, nor Wind, nor Storme, is able to
 remove,
Truft to that fure celeftiall rocke, that refts in glorious
 throne,
That hath bene, is, and muft be ftil, our anker hold alone.
  The world is but a vanitie,
  In heaven feeke we our furetie.

     The Paradife of Daynty Devifes.
     Fol. 18, 44. figned F. K.

CHURCH

CHURCH MONUMENTS.

WHILE that my Soul repairs to her devotion,
    Here I intomb my flesh, that it betimes
May take acquaintance of this heap of duft ;
To which the blaft of Death's inceffant motion,
Fed with the exhalation of our crimes,
Drives all at laft, therefore I gladly truft

My body to the School, that it may learn
To fpell his elements, and finds his birth
Written in dufty herauldry and lines.
Which diffolution fure doth beft difcern,
Comparing duft with duft, and earth with earth.
Thefe laugh at jeat, and marble put for figns,

To fever the good fellowfhip of duft,
And fpoil the meeting. What fhall point out them,
When they fhall bow, and kneel, and fall down flat
To kifs thofe heaps, which now they have in truft ?
Dear flefh, while I do pray, learn here thy ftem
And true defcent: that when thou fhalt grow fat,

And

And wanton in thy cravings, thou mayft know,
That flefh is but the glafs which holds the duft
That meaufures all our time ; which alfo fhall
Be crumbled into duft, mark here below,
How tame thefe afhes are, how free from luft,
That thou may'ft fit thyfelf againft thy fall.

The Temple, by **G.** Herbert,

Edit. 1709, p 56.

AGAINST FOREIGN LUXURY.

AND now ye Britifh fwaines (whofe harmeleffe fheepe
Then all the worlds befide I joy to keepe)
Which fpread on every plaine, and hilly would,
Fleeces no leffe efteem'd then that of gold,
For whofe exchange one Indy jems of price,
The other gives you of her choiceft fpice,
And well fhe may ; but we unwife, the while,
Leffen the glory of our fruitfull Ifle :
Making thofe nations thinke we foolifh are,
For bafer drugs to vent our richer ware,
Which (fave the bringer) never profit man,
Except the Sexten and Phyfitian.
And whether change of clymes, or what it be,
That proves our marainers mortalitie,

Such

Such expert men are fpent for fuch bad fares
As might have made us Lords of what is theirs.
Stay, ftay at home, ye nobler fpirits, and prife
Your lives more high then fuch bafe trumperies ;
Forbeare to fetch; and they 'le goe neere to fue,
And at your owne dores offer them to you ;
Or have their woods and plaines fo overgrowne
With poyfnous weeds, roots, gums, and feeds unknowne ;
That they would hire fuch weeders as you be
To free their land from fuch fertilitie.
Their fpices hot their nature beft indures,
But 'twill impayre and much diftemper yours.
What our owne foyle affords befits us beft ;
And long and long, for ever may we reft
Needleffe of help ! and may this Ifle alone
Furnifh all other lands, and this land none!

> Brit. Paft. B. II. Song IV.
> by W. Browne. Thomp.
> Edit.

OF THE COURTIER'S LIFE.

MYNE own John Poines, fins ye delight to know
   The caufes why that homeward I me draw,
And flee the preafe of Courtes, wherefo they goe,
Rather then to live thrall under the awe
Of lordly lookes, wrapped within my cloke,
To will and luft learning to fet a law ;
It is not, that becaufe I ftorme or mocke
The power of them, whom Fortune here hath lent
Charge over us, of right to ftrike the ftroke ;
But true it is, that I have always ment
Lefs to efteeme them, then the common fort,
Of outward thinges that judge in their entent,
Without regarde, what inward doth refort :
I graunt, fome time of Glory that the fyre,
Doth touch my heart, me lift not to report :
Blame by honour and honour to defyre.
But how may I this honour now attaine,
That cannot dye the colour blacke a lyer ?
My Poynes, I cannot frame my tune to fayn,
To cloke the truth, for praife, without defert,
Of them that lift all vice for to retayne :
I cannot honour them that fet theyr part
With Venus and Bacchus all their life long ;
Nor hold my peace of them, although I fmart.
I cannot crouche nor knele to fuch a wronge,

To

As Dronkennefs good fellowfhip to call,
The frendly foe with his faire double face,
Say he is gentle, and curties therewithall;
Affirme that Favill hath a goodly grace
In eloquence; and cruelty to name,
Zeale of Juftice; and change in time and place:
And he that fuffereth offence without blame,
Call him pitefull, and him true and playne,
That rayleth rechlefs unto eche man's fhame,
Say he is rude, that cannot lye and fayne;
The lecher a lover, and tyranny
To be right of a Prince's raigne.
I cannot I, no no, it will not be.
This is the caufe that I could never yet,
Hang on their fleeves the weigh (as thou maift fee)
A chippe of chaunce, more than a pound of wit:
This makes me at home to hunt and hawke,
And in foul weather at my book to fit,
In froft and fnow, then with my bowe ftalke,
No man doth marke wherefo I ryde or goe,
In lufty leas at libertie I walke;
And of thefe newes I fele no weale no woe,
Save that a clogge doth hang yett at my hele,
No force for that, for that is ordered fo,
That I may leape both hedge and dyke full wele.
I am not now in France to judge the wyne,
With favery fauce thofe delicates to feele,
Nor yet in Spayne, where one muft him incline,
Rather then to be, outwardly to feme,
I meddle not with wittes that be fo fyne,
Nor Flanders chere lettes to my fight to deme,
Of black and white, nor takes my wittes away;
With beaftlinefs, fuch doe thofe beaftes efteme!
Nor I am not, where truth is geven in pay
For money, pryfon and treafon; of fome
A common practice ufed night and daye:

But

But I am here in Kent and Chriftendome,
Among the Mufes, where I reade and ryme,
Where if thou lift, mine own John Poynes to come,
Thou fhalt be judge, how I do fpende my tyme.

Sir Thomas Wyat.
Tottel's Edit.

The Pleafures of Literary Retirement.

MY free-borne Mufe will not, like Danae, be
   Wonnne with bafe droffe to clip with flavery;
Nor lend her choifer balme to worthleffe men,
Whofe names would die but for fome hired pen;
No : if I praife, Vertue fhall draw me to it,
And not a bafe procurement make me doe it.
What now I fing is but to paffe away
A tedious houre, as fome mufitians play;
Or make an other my owne griefes bemone;
Or to be leaft alone when moft alone,
In this can I, as oft as I will chufe,
Hug fweet Content by my retyred mufe,
And in a ftudy finde as much to pleafe
As others in the greateft Palaces.
Each man that lives (according to his powre)
On what he loves beftowes an idle howre;
Inftead of hounds that make the wooded hils
Talke in a hundred voyces to the rils,
I like the pleafing cadence of a line
Strucke by the concert of the facred Nine.
In lieu of Hawkes, the raptures of my foule
Tranfcend their pitch and bafer earths controule.
For running horfes, Contemplation flyes
With quickeft fpeed to winne the greateft prize.

D 3

For

For courtly dancing, I can take more pleafure
To heare a verfe keepe time and equall meafure.
For winning riches, feeke the beft directions
How I may well fubdue mine owne affections.
For rayfing ftately pyles for heyres to come,
Here in this poem I erect my toombe.
And time may be fo kinde, in thefe weake lines
To keepe my name enroll'd, paft his, that fhines
In guilded marble, or in brazen leaves :
Since verfe preferves when ftone and braffe deceives.
Or if (as worthleffe) Time not lets it live
To thofe full days which others Mufes give,
Yet I am fure I fhall be heard and fung
Of moft fevereft eld, and kinder young
Beyond my dayes, and maugre Envye's ftrife
Adde to my name fome houres beyond my life,
Such, of the Mufes, are the able powres,
And, fince with them I fpent my vacant houres,
I finde nor hawke, nor hound, nor other thing,
Turnyes nor revels, (pleafures for a King)
Yeeld more delight ; for I have oft poffeft
As much in this as all in all the reft,
And that without expence, when others oft
With their undoings have their pleafures bought.

Brit. Paft. B. II. Song IV.
by W. Browne.

ELEGIES

ELEGIES and EPITAPHS.

On the Death of Mrs. Elizabeth Filmer, an Elegiacall Epitaph.

Y O U that fhall live awhile before
　Old Time tyr's, and is no more ;
When that this ambitious ftone
Stoopes low as what it tramples on ;
Know that in that Age when Sinne
Gave the World law, and govern'd Queene,
A Virgin liv'd, that ftill put
White thoughts, though out of fafhion ;
That trac't the ftars fpite of report,
And durft be good, though chidden fort :
Of fuch a foule ————— Heav'n
Repented what it thus had giv'n ;
For finding equall happy man,
Th' impatient Pow'rs fnatcht it agen ;
Thus chafte as th' ayre whither fhee's fled,
She making her celeftiall bed
In her warme alabafter lay
As cold as in this houfe of clay ;

Nor

Nor were the rooms unfit to feaſt
Or circumſcribe this Angel-gueſt ;
The radiant gemme was brightly ſet
In as divine a carkanet ;
For which the clearer was not knowne,
Her minde, or her complexion :
Such an everlaſting grace,
Such a beatiſick face
Incloyſters here this narrow floore
That poſſeſt all hearts before.
Bleſt and bewayl'd in death and birth !
The ſmiles and teares of Heav'n and Earth !
Virgins at each ſtep are afeard,
Filmer is ſhot by which they ſteer'd,
Their ſtar extinct, their beauty dead
That the yong world to honour led ;
But ſee ! the rapid ſpheres ſtand ſtill,
And tune themſelves unto her will.
Thus, although this Marble muſt,
As all things crumble into duſt,
And though you finde this faire-built Tombe
Aſhes, as what lyes in its wombe ;
Yet her Saint-like name ſhall ſhine
A living glory to this ſhrine,
And her eternall fame be read,
When all, but very Vertue's dead.

Lucaſta. &c. &c.
by Richard Lovelace, Eſq;
Lond. 1649. Ed.

EPITAPH

EPITAPH on the LADY MARY

VILLERS.

THE Lady Mary Villers lyes
   Under this ftone; with weeping eyes
The Parents that firft gave her birth,
And their fad Friends lay'd her in earth:
If any of them (Reader) were
Knowne unto thee, fhed a teare,
Or if thyfelfe poffeffe a gemme,
As deare to thee, as this to them;
Though a ftranger to this place,
Bewayle in theirs, thine owne hard cafe
For thou perhaps at thy returne
Mayeft find thy Darling in an urne.

Poems by Tho. Carew Efq.
Lond. 1640, p. 90.

ON

On the EARL of DORSET'S DEATH

LET no prophane ignoble foot tread here,
  This hallowed piece of Earth, Dorſet lyes there:
A ſmall poor relique of a noble ſpirit,
Free as the aire, and ample as his merit:
A ſoul refin'd, no proud forgetting Lord
But mindfull of mean names, and of his word:
Who lov'd men for his honour, not his ends,
And had the nobleſt way of getting friends
By loving firſt, and yet who knew the Court,
But underſtood it better by report
Then praCtiſe: he nothing took from thence
But the King's favour for his recompence.
Who for Religion, or his Countrey's good,
Neither his honour valued, nor his blood.
Rich in the World's opinion, and men's praiſe,
And full in all we could deſire, but dayes,
He that is warn'd of this, and ſhall forbeare
To vent a ſigh for him, or ſhed a teare,
May he live long ſcorn'd and unpitied fall,
And want a Mourner at his funerall.

Certain Elegant Poems.
Written by Dr. Corbet Biſhop
of Norwich, 1647. Ed. Lond. p. 51.

O N

On the DEATH of a YOUNG LADY.

FOND wight, who dreamſt of Greatneſs, Glory, State,
And worlds of pleaſures, honours to deviſe,
Awake, learne here that how thou art not great,
Nor glorious ; by this Monument turne wiſe.

One it enſhrineth ſprung of ancient ſtemm,
And (if that bloud nobility can make)
Frome which ſome Kings have not diſdain'd to take
Their proud deſcent, a rare and matchleſs gemm.

A beauty here it holds alas, too faſt !
Than which no blooming roſe was more refin'd,
Nor morning's bluſh more radiant ever ſhin'd,
Ah! too too like to Morne and Roſe at laſt.

It holds her who in Wit's aſcendant far
Did yeares and ſex tranſcend, to whom the Heaven
More vertue than to all this age had given,
For Vertue meteor turn'd, when ſhe a ſtar.

Faire

Faire Mirth, ſweet Converſation, Modeſty,
And what thoſe Kings of numbers did conceive
By Muſes Nine, and Graces more than three,
Lye cloſ'd within the compaſſe of this grave.
  Thus Death all earthly glories doth confound,
  Loe ! how much worth a little duſt doth bound.

       Drummond's Poems, 8vo.
       1656, p. 198.

An ELEGY on the Death of PHILARETE,
i. e. Mr. THO. MANWOOD, the Author's
Friend, and Son of Sir PETER MAN-
WOOD, Knight.

UNDER an aged oke was Willy laid,
  Willy, the lad who whilome made the rockes
To ring with joy whilſt on his pipe he plaid,
And from their maſter's wood the neighb'ring flocks ;
    But now o'recome with dolors deepe
     That nie his heart-ſtrings rent :
    Ne car'd he for his ſilly ſheepe,
     Ne car'd for merriment.
    But chang'd his wonted walkes
     For uncouth paths unknowne,
    Where none but trees might hear his plaints,
     And eccho rue his mone.

            Autumne

Autumne it was, when droopt the fweeteft floures,
And rivers (fwolne with pride) ore-look'd the banks,
Poore grew the day of Summer's golden houres,
And void of fap ftood Ida's cedar-rankes,
  The pleafant meadows fadly lay
   In chill and cooling fweats,
  By rifing fountaines, or as they
   Fear'd Winter's waftfull threats.
  Againft the broad-fpread oke,
   Each wind in furie beares ;
  Yet fell their leaves not halfe fo faft
   As did the Shepheard's teares.

As was his feate fo was his gentle heart,
Meeke and dejected, but his thoughts as hie
As thofe aye-wandring lights, who both impart
Their beames on us, and heaven ftill beautifie.
  Sad was his looke (O heavy fate !
   That fwaine fhould be fo fad,
  Whofe merry notes the forlorne mate
   With greateft pleafure clad)
  Broke was his tunefull pipe
   That charm'd the chriftall floods.
  And thus his griefe tooke airie wings
   And flew about the woods.

" Day, thou art too officious in thy place,
And Night too fparing of a wifhed ftay,
Yee wand'ring lampes ; O be ye fixt a fpace !
Some other Hemifphere grace with your ray.
  Great Phœbus ! Daphne is not heere,
   Nor Hyacinthus faire ;
  Phœbe, Endimion, and thy deere
   Hath long fince cleft the aire,
  But ye have furely feene
   (Whom we in forrow miffe)
  A fwaine whom Phœbe thought her love
   And Titan deemed his.
        ' But

5

But he is gone ; then inwards turn your light,
Behold him there ; here never fhall you more,
O're-hang this fad plaine with eternall night !
Or change the gaudy greene fhe whilome wore
  To fenny blacke.   Hyperion great
  To afhy paleneffe turne her !
Greene well befits a lover's heate,
  But blacke befeemes a mourner.
Yet neither this thou can'ft,
  Nor fee his fecond birth,
His brightneffe blinds thine eye more now,
  Then thine did his on earth.

Let not a fhepheard on our hapleffe plaines,
Tune notes of glee, as ufed were of yore :
For Philarete is dead, let mirthfull ftraines
With Philarete ceafe for evermore !
  And if a fellow fwaine doe live
  A niggard of his teares;
  The fhepheardeffes all will give
  To ftore him, part of theirs.
  Or I would lend him fome,
  But that the ftore I have
Will all be fpent before I pay
  The debt I owe his grave.

O what is left can make me leave to mone !
Or what remains but doth increafe it more ?
Looke on his fheepe ; alas ! their mafter's gone.
Looke on the place where we two heretofore
  With locked armes have vow'd our love,
  (Our love which time fhall fee
  In fhepheards fongs for ever move,
  And grace their harmony)
  It folitarie feemes.
  Behold our flowrie beds ;
  Their beauties fade, and violets
  For forow hang their heads.

'Tis not a cypreſſe bough, a count'nance ſad,
A mourning garment, wailing elegie,
A ſtanding herſe in ſable veſture clad,
A toombe built to his name's eternitie.
 Although the ſhepheards all ſhould ſtrive
  By yearly obſequies,
 And vow to keepe thy fame alive
  In ſpite of Deſtinies,
 That can ſuppreſſe my griefe;
  All theſe, and more may be,
 Yet all in vain to recompence
  My greateſt loſſe of thee.

Cypreſſe may fade, the countenance be chang'd,
A garment rot, an elegie forgotten,
A herſe 'mongſt irreligious rites be ranged,
A tombe pluckt down, or els through age be rotten:
 All things th' unpartial hand of Fate
  Can raſe out with a thought:
 Theſe have a ſev'ral fixed date,
  Which ended, turn to nought.
 Yet ſhall my trueſt cauſe
  Of ſorrow firmely ſtay,
 When theſe effects the wings to Time
  Shall fanne and ſweepe away.

Looke as a ſweet roſe fairely budding forth
·Bewrayes her beauties to the enamour'd morne,
Untill ſome keene blaſt from the envious North
Killes the ſweet bud that was but newly borne,
 Or els her rareſt ſmels delighting
  Make her herſelfe betray
 Some white and curious hand inviting
  To pluck her thence away.
 So ſtands my mournfull caſe,
  For had he been leſſe good,
 Yet (uncorrupt) he had kept the ſtocke
  Whereon he fairly ſtood.

           Yet

Yet though fo long he liv'd not as he might,
He had the time appointed to him given.
Who liveth but the fpace of one poor night,
His birth, his youth, his age is in that even.
　　Whoever doth the period fee
　　　Of dayes by Heav'n forth plotted,
　　Dyes full of age, as well as he
　　　That had more yeares allotted.
　　In fad tones then my verfe
　　　Shall with inceffant teares
　　Bemoane my haplcffe loffe of him
　　　And not his want of yeares.

In deepeft paffions of my grief-fwolne breaft
(Sweete Soule!) this onely comfort feizeth me,
That fo few yeeres fhould make thee fo much bleft,
And gave fuch wings to reach eternitie.
　　Is this to die? no, as a fhip
　　　Well built, with eafy wind
　　A lazy hulk doth farre outftrip,
　　　And fooneft harbour find:
　　So Philarete fled,
　　　Quicke was his paffage given,
　　When others muft have longer time
　　　To make them fit for Heaven.

Then not for thee thefe briny teares are fpent,
But as the Nightingale againft the breere,
'Tis for myfelfe I moane, and doe lament,
Not that thou left'ft the world, but left'ft me here:
　　Here, where without thee all delights
　　　Faile of their pleafing powre:
　　All glorious daies feeme ugly nights,
　　　Methinks no Aprill fhowre
　　Embroder fhould the earth,
　　　But briny teares diftill,
　　Since Flora's beauties fhall no more
　　　Be honour'd by thy quill.

And ye his fheepe (in token of his lacke)
Whilome the faireft flocke on all the plaine :
Yeane never lambe, but be it cloath'd in blacke.
Ye fhady ficcamours ! when any fwaine,
  To carve his name upon your rind
   Doth come, where his doth ftand,
  Shed drops, if he be fo unkind
   To raze it with his hand.
  And thou, my loved Mufe,
   No more fhould'ft numbers move,
  But that his name fhould ever live,
   And after death my love.

This faid, he figh'd, and with o're drowned eyes
Gaz'd on the Heavens for what he mift on Earth ;
Then from the earth, full gladly gan arife
As far from future hope, as prefent mirth,
  Unto his cote with heavy pace
   As ever forrow trode,
  He went, with mind no more to trace
   Where mirthful fwaines abode,
  And as he fpent the day
   The night he paft alone ;
  Was never Shepheard lov'd more deere,
   Nor made a truer mone.

      The Shepheard's Pipe,
      Eclogue 4, by W. Browne.

An E L E G Y on the late Lord W I L L I A M H O W A R D, Baron of E F F I N G H A M, dead the 10th of December, 1615.

I Did not know thee, Lord, nor doe I ſtrive
   To winne acceſſe, or grace, with Lords alive.
The dead I ſerve, from whence nor faction can
Move me, nor favour ; nor a greater man.
To whom no vice commends me, nor bribe ſent,
From whom no penance warnes, nor portion ſpent,
To theſe I dedicate as much of me.
As I can ſpare from my owne huſbandry :
And 'till ghoſts walke, as they were wont to doe,
I trade for ſome, and doe theſe errants too ;
But firſt I doe enquire, and am aſſur'd,
What tryals in their journies they endur'd,
What certainties of honour and of worth,
Their moſt uncertaine life-times have brought forth :
And who ſo did leaſt hurt of this ſmall ſtore,
He is my patron, dy'd he rich or poore.
Firſt I will know of Fame (after his peace,
When Flattery and Envy both doe ceaſe)
Who rul'd his actions, Reaſon, or my Lord ?
Did the whole man relie upon a word,
A badge of title, or above all chance,
Seem'd he as ancient as his cogniſance ?
What did he ? acts of mercy, and refraine
Oppreſſion in himſelfe, and in his traine ?

Was

Was his effentiall table full as free
As boafts and invitations ufe to be?
There if his ruffet-friend did chance to dine,
Whether his fatten-man would fill him wine?
Did he thinke perjury as lov'd a finne,
Himfelfe forfworne, as if his flave had beene?
Did he feeke regular pleafures? was he knowne
Juft hufband of one wife, and fhe his owne?
Did he give freely without paufe or doubt,
And read petitions, ere they were worne out?
Or fhould his well-deferving client afke,
Would he beftow a Tilting or a Mafke
To keepe need vertuous? and that done not feare
What Lady damn'd him for his abfence there?
Did he attend the Court for no man's fall?
Wore he the ruine of no Hofpitall?
And when he did his rich apparell don,
'Ut he no widow, nor an orphan on?
Did he love fimple vertue for the thing?
The King for no refpect but for the King?
But above all, did his Religion wait
Upon God's Throne, or on the Chaire of State?
He that is guiltie of no Quære here,
Out-lafts his epitaph, oulives his heire.
But there is none fuch, none fo little bad,
Who but this negative goodneffe ever had?
Of fuch a Lord we may expect the birth,
He's rather in the wombe than on the earth.
And 'twere a crime in fuch a publike fate,
For one to live well and degenerate;
And therefore I am angry, when a name
Comes to upbraid the world like Effingham.
Nor was it modeft in thee to depart
To thy eternall home, where now thou art,
Ere thy reproach was ready; or to dye,
Ere cuftome had prepar'd thy calumny.

Eight dayes have paſt ſince thou haſt paid thy debt
'To ſinne, and not a libell ſtirring yet,
Courtiers that ſcoffe by Patent, ſilent ſit,
And have no uſe of ſlander or of wit ;
But (which is monſtrous) though againſt the tide,
The watermen have neither rayld nor lide.
Of good and bad there's no diſtinction known,
For in thy praiſe the good and bad are one.
It ſeemes we all are covetous of Fame,
And hearing what a purchaſe of good name
Thou lately mad'ſt, are carefull to encreaſe
Our title by the holding of ſome leaſe
From thee our Land-Lord, and for that th' whole crue
Speake now like tenants ready to renew ;
It were too ſad to tell thy pedegree,
Death hath diſorder'd all, miſplacing thee,
Whilſt now thy Herauld in his line of heires
Blots out thy name, and fills the ſpace with teares.
And thus hath conqu'ring death, or nature rather,
Made thee, prepoſtrous, ancient to thy father,
Who grieves th' art ſo, and like a glorious light
Shines ore thy Hearſe ; he therefore that would write
And blaze thee thoroughly, may at once ſay all
Here lies the Anchor of our Admirall.
Let others write for glory or reward,
Truth is well paid, when ſhe is ſung and heard.

Corbet's Poems.
p. 22, 1647. Ed. Lond

ELEG'

ELEGY on DR. AILMER.

NO, no, he is not dead; the mouth of Fame,
 Honor's fhrill Herald, would preferve his name,
And make it live in fpite of death and duft,
Were there no other heaven, no other truft.
He is not dead : the facred Nine deny,
The foule that merits fame, fhould ever dye;
He lives ; and when the lateft breath of fame
Shall want her trumpe to glorify a name,
He fhall furvive, and thefe felfe-clofed eyes,
That now lie flumbring in the duft fhall rife,
And fill'd with endleffe glory, fhall enjoy
The perfect vifion of eternall joy.

13 El. by F. Quarles.
Subjoined to Sion's Elegies,
1630.—Ed.

On

On the Death of a SCOTCH NOBLEMAN

FAME, regifter of Time,
Write in thy fcrowle, that I
Of Wifdome lover, and fweet Poefie,
Was cropped in my prime:
And ripe in worth, though greene in yeares did dye.

> Drummond, p. 203.
> Small 8vo. Ed.

MORS TUA.

METHINKES, I fee the nimble aged Sire
Paffe fwiftly by, with feet unapt to tire;
Upon his head an Hower-glaffe he weares,
And in his wrinkled hand a fythe he beares,
(Both inftruments, to take the lives from men)
Th' one fhewes with what, the other fheweth when.
Methinkes, I heare the dolefull paffing-bell,
Setting an onfet on his louder knell;
(This moody mufick of impartiall death
Who dances after dances out of breath).

Methinkes I fee my deareſt friends lament,
With ſighes and teares, and wofull dryrimeṁt,
My tender wife and children ſtanding by.
Dewing the Death-bed, whereupon I lye :
Methinkes, I hear a voice (in ſecret) ſay,   ·
" Thy glaſſe is runne, and thou muſt dye to-day."

Pentelogia, by F. Quarles.
Lond. 1630.

Upon the Death of C H A R L E S the Firſt.
Written with the Point of his Sword.

GREAT, good, and juſt ! could I but rate
G My grief to thy too rigid fate,
I'd weep the world to ſuch a ſtrain,
As it ſhould deluge once again.
But ſince thy loud-tongu'd blood demands ſupplies,
More from Briareus hands, than Argus eyes,
Il'e ſing thee obſequies with trumpet ſounds
And write thy Epitaph in blood and wounds.

MONTROSE.

Printed amongſt Poems by J. Cleaveland,
1665, Lond. Ed. See likewiſe, A
Choice Collection of Comic and Se-
rious Scots Poems. Edinburgh 1713.

AN ELEGY

Upon the Honourable HENRY CAMBELL,

Sonne to the Earle of A R.

IT's falſe Arithmaticke to ſay thy breath
  Expir'd to ſoone, or irreligious death
Prophan'd thy holy youth ; for if thy yeares
Be number'd by thy vertues or our teares,
Thou didſt the old Methuſalem outlive.
Though Time, but twenty yeares account can give
Of thy abode on earth, yet every houre
Of thy brave youth by vertue's wondrous powre
Was lengthen'd to a yeare, each well-ſpent day
Keepes young the body, but the ſoule makes gray,
Such miracies workes goodneſſe ; and behind
Thou 'aſt left to us ſuch ſtories of thy minde
Fit for example ; that when them we read,
We envy Earth the treaſure of the dead.
Why doe the ſinfull riot and ſurvive
The feavers of their ſurfets ? why alive
Is yet diſorder'd Greatneſſe, and all they
Who the looſe lawes of their wilde blood obey ?
Why lives the gameſter, who doth blacke the night
With cheats and imprecations ? Why is light

Looked

Looked on by thofe whofe breath may poifon it :
Who fold the vigor of their ftrength and wit
To buy difeafes : and thou, who faire truth
And vertue didft adore, loft in thy youth ?
  But Ile not queftion fate : Heaven doth conveigh
Thofe firft from the darke prifon of their clay
Who are moft fit for Heaven.   Thou in warre
Hadft tane degrees, thofe dangers felt, which are
The props on which peace fafely doft fubfift,
And through the cannons blew and horrid mift
Hadft brought her light ; and now wert fo compleat
That naught but death did want to make thee great.
  Thy death was timely then bright foule to thee,
And in thy fate thou fuffer'dft not ; 'twas we
Who dyed rob'd of thy life : in whofe increafe
Of reall glory both in warre and peace,
We all did fhare : and thou away we feare
Didft with thee, the whole ftocke of honour beare.
Each then be his own mourner : we'll to thee
Write hymnes, upon the world an elegie.

Caftara, 1640. Edit.
by W. Habington, Efq.

THE

THE EXEQUY.

ACCEPT thou Shrine of My dead Saint
   Infteed of dirges this complaint;
And for fweet flowres to crown thy hearfe,
Receive a ftrew of weeping verfe
From thy griev'd friend, whom thou might'ft fee
Quite melted into tears for thee.
   Dear lofs! fince thy untimely fate
My tafk hath been to meditate
On thee, on thee: thou art the book,
The library whereon I look
Though almoft blind, for thee (lov'd clay)
I languifh out not live the day,
Ufing no other exercife
But what I practife with mine eyes:
By which wet glaffes I find out
How lazily Time creeps about
To one that mourns: this, onely this
My exercife and bus'nefs is:
So I compute the weary houres
With fighs diffolved into fhow'res.
   Nor wonder if my time go thus
Backward and moft prepofterous;
Thou haft benighted me, thy fet,
This Eve of blacknefs did beget,
Who waft my day, (though overcaft
Before thou hadft thy noontide paft)

And I remember muſt in tears,
Thou ſcarce hadſt ſeen ſo many years
As day tells houres by thy clear Sun
My love and fortune firſt did run ;
But thou wilt never more appear
Folded within my hemiſphear,
Since both thy light and motion
Like a fled ſtar is fall'n and gon,
'And twixt me and my ſoules dear wiſh
The earth now interpoſed is,
Which ſuch a ſtrange eclipſe doth make
As ne're was read in Almanake.

I could allow thee for a time
To darken me and my ſad clime
Were it a month, a year, or ten,
I would thy exile live till then ;
And all that ſpace my mirth adjourn,
So thou would'ſt promiſe to return ;
And putting off thy aſhy ſhrowd
At length diſperſe this ſorrow's cloud.

But woe is me ! the longeſt date
Too narrow is to calculate
Theſe empty hopes : never ſhall I
Be ſo much bleſt as to deſcry
A glimpſe of thee, till that day come
Which ſhall the earth to cinders doome,
And a fierce feaver muſt calcine
The body of this world like thine,
(My little world !) that fit of fire
Once off, our bodies ſhall aſpire
To our ſoules bliſs : then we ſhall riſe,
And view ourſelves with cleerer eyes
In that calm region, where no night
Can hide us from each others ſight.

Mean m , thou haſt her Earth : much good
May my harm do thee, ſince it ſtood

With

With Heaven's will I might not call
Her longer mine, I give thee all
My ſhort-liv'd right and intereſt
In her, whom living I lov'd beſt:
With a moſt free and bounteous grief,
I give thee what I could not keep.
Be kind to her, and prethee look
'Thou write into thy doomſ-day book
Each parcel of this Rarity
Which in thy caſket ſhrin'd doth ly :
See that thou make thy reck'ning ſtreight,
And yield her back again by weight ;
For thou muſt audit on thy truſt
Each graine and atome of this duſt,
As thou wilt anſwer *Him* that lent,
Not gave thee my dear monument.
So cloſe the ground, and 'bout her ſhade
Black curtains draw, my Bride is laid.

Sleep on, my Love, in thy cold bed
Never to be diſquieted !
My laſt good night ! thou wilt not wake
Till I thy fate ſhall overtake :
Till age, or grief, or ſickneſs muſt
Marry my body to that duſt
It ſo much loves ; and fill the room
My heart keeps empty in thy tomb.
Stay for me there ; I will not faile
To meet thee in that hollow vale.
And think not much of my delay :
I am already on the way,
And follow thee with all the ſpeed
Deſire can make, or ſorrows breed.
Each minute is a ſhort degree,
And ev'ry houre a ſtep towards thee.
At night when I betake to reſt,
Next morn I riſe neerer my weſt

4

Of life, almoſt by eight houres faile,
Then when ſleep breath'd his drowſie gale.
Thus from the Sun my bottom ſtears
And my dayes compaſs downward bears:
Nor labour I to ſtemme the tide
Through which to thee I ſwiftly glide.
'Tis true, with ſhame and grief I yield,
Thou like the vann firſt took'ſt the field,
And gotten haſt the victory
In thus adventuring to dy
Before me, whoſe more years might crave
A juſt precedence in the grave.
But heark! my pulſe like a ſoft drum
Beats my approach, tells Thee I come;
And ſlow howerè my marches be,
I ſhall at laſt ſit down by Thee.
The thought of this bids me go on,
And wait my diſſolution
With hope and comfort, Dear (forgive
The crime) I am content to live
Divided, with but half a heart,
Till we ſhall meet and never part.

Dr. King's Poems. p. 57.

Of

Of my deare Sonne, GERVASE BEAUMONT.

C A N I, who have for others oft compil'd
  The fongs of Death, forget my fweeteft child,
Which like a flow'r crufht, with a blaft is dead,
And ere full time hangs downe his fmiling head,
Expecting with cleare hope to live anew,
Among the Angels fed with heav'nly dew?
We have this figne of joy, that many dayes,
While on the earth his ftruggling fpirit ftayes,
The name of Jefus in his mouth contains
His onely food, his fleepe, his eafe from paines.
O may that found be rooted in my mind
Of which in him fuch ftrong effect I find.
Deare Lord, receive my Sonne, whofe winning love
To me was like a friendfhip, farre above
The courfe of nature, or his tender age,
Whofe lookes could all my bitter griefes affwage;
Let his pure foule ordain'd fev'n yeeres to be
In that fraile body, which was part of me,
Remaine my pledge in Heav'n, as fent to fhew,
How to this port at ev'ry ftep I goe.

Bofworth Field, with other
Poems, by Sir John Beaumont.
Lond. 1629. Ed.

The

The Funerals of the Honourable, my beſt friend and Kinſman, GEORGE TALBOT Eſq;

G O E ſtop the ſwift-wing'd moments in their flight
To their yet unknowne coaſt, goe hinder night
From its approach on day, and force day riſe
From the faire Eaſt of ſome bright beauties eyes :
Elſe vaunt not the proud miracle of verſe.
It hath no powre, for mine from his blacke herſe
Redeemes not Talbot, who could as the breath
Of Winter, coffin'd lyes ; ſilent as Death,
Stealing on th' Anch'rit, who even wants an eare
To breath into his ſoft expiring prayer.
For had thy life beene by thy virtues ſpun
Out to a length, thou hadſt out-liv'd the Sunne
And cloſ'd the world's great eye : or were not all
Our wonders fiction, from thy funerall
Thou hadſt received new life, and liv'd to be
The conqueror o'er Death, inſpir'd by me.
But all we poets glory in is vaine
And empty triumph : Art cannot regaine
One poore houre loſt, nor reſkew a ſmall flye
By a foole's finger deſtinate to dye.
Live then in thy true life (great ſoule) for ſet
At liberty by Death thou oweſt no debt

T^v

T' exacting Nature : live, freed from the fport
Of time and fortune in yond' ftarry court
A glorious potentate, while we below
But fafhion wayes to mitigate our woe.
We follow campes, and to our hopes propofe
Th' infulting victor ; not remembring thofe
Difmemberd trunkes who gave him victory
By a loath'd fate: we covetous merchants be
And to our aymes pretend treafure and fway,
Forgetfull of the treafons of the fea,
The fhootings of a wounded confcience
We patiently fuftaine to ferve our fence
With a fhort pleafure ; fo we empire gaine
And rule the fate of buifneffe, the fad paine
Of action we contemne, and the affright
Which with pale vifions ftill attends our night.
Our joyes falfe apparitions, but our feares
Are certain prophecies, and till our eares
Reach that celeftiall mufique, which thine now
So cheerefully receive, we muft allow
No comfort to our griefes : from which to be
Exempted, is in death to follow thee.

Caftara. 1640. Lond. E
by W. Habington.

O

On two Children dying of one difeafe, and buried in one grave.

Brought forth in forrow, and bred up in care,
Two tender Children here entombed are :
One place, one Sire, one Womb their being gave,
They had one mortal Sicknefs, and one grave,
And though they cannot number many years
In their account, yet with their Parents tears
This comfort mingles; though their dayes were few
They fcarcely finne, but never forrow knew :
So that they well might boaft, they carry'd hence
What riper ages lofe, their innocence,
    You pretty loffes, that revive the fate
Which in your Mother Death did antedate,
O let my high-fwoln grief diftill on you
The faddeft drops of a Parentall dew :
You afk no other dower then what my eyes
Lay out on your untimely exequies :
When once I have difcharg'd that mournfull fkore,
Heav'n hath decreed you ne're fhall coft me more,
Since you releafe and quit my borrow'd truft,
By taking this inheritance of duft.

Dr. King's Poems, p. 60.

To the Memory of BEN JONSON, Laureat.

FATHER of Poets, though thine own great day
 Struck from thyfelf, fcorns that a weaker ray
Should twine in luftre with it, yet my flame
Kindled from thine, flies upward towards thy name:
For in the acclamation of the lefs
There's piety, though from it no accefs:
And though my ruder thoughts make me of thofe
Who hide and cover what they fhould difclofe,
Yet where the luftre's fuch, he makes it feen
Better to fome that draws the veil between.
  And what can more be hop'd, fince that divine
Free filling fpirit takes its flight with thine?
Men may have fury, but no raptures now,
Like Witches charm, yet not know whence, nor how,
And through diftemper grown not ftrong, but fierce,
Inftead of writing, only rave in verfe;
Which when by thy laws judg'd, 'twill be confeft
'Twas not to be infpir'd, but be poffeft.
  Where fhall we find a Mufe like thine, that can
So well prefent, and fhew man unto man,
That each one finds his twin, and thinks thy art
Extends not to the geftures, but the heart?
Where one fo fhewing life to life, that we
Think thou taught'ft cuftome, and not cuftome thee;

Manners

Manners were themes, and to thy ſcenes ſtill flow
In the ſame ſtream, and are their comments now ;
Theſe times thus living o'er thy models, we
Think them not ſo much Wit, as Prophecie;
And though we know the character, nay and ſwear
A Sybil's finger hath been buſie there.
Things common thou ſpeak'ſt proper, which though known
For publike, ſtamp'd by Thee, grow thence thine own;
Thy thought's ſo ordered, ſo expreſs'd, that we
Conclude that thou didſt not diſcourſe, but ſee :
Language ſo maſter'd that thy numerous feet
Laden with genuine words do alwaies meet
Each in his art, nothing unfit doth fall,
Shewing the Poet, like the wiſe men, all
Thine equall ſkill thus wreſting nothing, made
Thy pen ſeem not ſo much to write, as trade.
   That life, that Venus of all things, which we
Conceive or ſhew, proportion'd Decency,
Is not found ſcatter'd in thee here or there,
But like the ſoul is wholly every where ;
No ſtrange perplexed maze doth paſs for plot,
Thou alwaies doſt unty, not cut the knot :
Thy labyrinth's doors are open'd by one thread,
Which tyes and runs through all that's done or ſaid ;
No Power comes down with learned hat or rod,
Wit onely and Contrivance is thy God.
   'Tis eaſie to gild gold, there's ſmall ſkill ſpent
Where ev'n the firſt rude maſs is ornament ;
Thy Muſe took harder metals, purg'd and boyl'd,
Labour'd and try'd, heated and beat, and toyl'd,
Sifted the droſs, fyl'd roughneſs, then gave dreſs,
Vexing rude ſubjects into comelineſs ;
Be it thy glory then that we may ſay,
Thou runeſt where the foot was hind'red by the way.
   Nor doſt thou powre out, but diſpence thy vein,
Skill'd when to ſpare, and when to entertain ;

Not

Not like our Wits. who into one piece do
Throw all that they can fay and their friends too :
Pumping themfelves for one Terms noife fo dry
As if they made their wills in poetry.
And fuch fpruce compofitions prefs the Stage
When men tranfcribe themfelves and not the Age;
Both forts of Plays are thus like pictures fhown,
Thine of the common life, theirs of their own.
    Thy models yet are not fo fram'd as we
May call them libels, and not imag'ry ;
No name on any bafis ; 'tis thy fkill
To ftrike the vice, but fpare the perfon ftill :
As He who when he faw the ferpent wreath'd
About his fleeping Son, and as he breath'd,
Drink in his foul, did fo the fhoot contrive,
To kill the beaft, but keep the child alive ;
So doft thou aime thy darts, which even when
They kill the poifons, do but wake the men.
Thy thunders thus but purge, and we endure
Thy lancings better than an other's cure ;
And juftly too, for th' Age grows more unfound
From the fool's balfam, than the wife man's wound.
  ' No rotten talk breaks for a laugh ; no Page
Commenc'd man by th' inftructions of thy Stage ;
No barganing line there ; no provoc'tive verfe;
Nothing but what Lucretia might rehearfe ;
No need to make good count'nance ill, and ufe
The plea of ftrict life for a loofer Mufe ;
No woman rul'd thy quill : we can defcry
No verfe born under any Cynthia's eye ;
Thy ftar was Judgement only and right Senfe,
Thy felf being to thyfelf an influence :
Stout Beauty is thy Grace ; ftern pleafures do
Prefent delights, but mingle horrours too :
Thy Mufe doth thus like Jove's fierce Girl appear,
With a fair hand, but grafping of a fpear.

Where are they now that cry thy lamp did drink
More Oyl than th' Author wine while he did think?
We do embrace their slander; thou hast writ
Not for difpatch, but fame; no market wit;
'Twas not thy care that it might pafs and fel,
But that it might endure, and be done well;
Nor would'ft thou venture it unto the ear,
Untill the file would not make fmooth, but wear:
Thy Verfe came feafon'd hence, and would not give;
Born not to feed the Author, but to live:
Whence 'mong the choicer Judges rofe a ftrife,
To make thee read a Claffick in thy life.
Thofe that do hence applaufe, and fuffrage beg,
Caufe they can Poems form upon one leg,
Write not to Time, but to the Poet's day;
There's difference between Fame and fudden pay:
Thefe men fing Kingdoms fals as if that Fate
Us'd the fame force to a Village and a State;
Thefe ferve Thyeftes' bloody Supper in,
As if it only had a fallad been;
Their Catilines are but fencers, whofe fights rife
Not to the fame of Battell but of Prize.
But thou ftill putft true paffions on; doft write
With the fame courage that tri'd captains fight;
Giv'ft the right blufh and colour unto things;
Low without creeping, high without lofs of wings;
Smooth, yet not weak, and by a thorough care,
Big without fwelling, without painting, fair;
They, wretches, while they cannot ftand to fit,
Wits are not, but materials of wit.
What though thy fearching Mufe did rake the duft
Of Time, and purge old metals of their ruft?
Is it no labour, no art, think they, to
Snatch fhipwracks from the deep as divers do?
And refcue jewels from the covetous fand,
Making the Sea's hid wealth adorn the Land?

What

What though thy culling Mufe did rob the ftore
Of Greek and Latine Gardens, to bring o'er
Plants to thy native foyl? their virtues were
Improv'd far more, by being planted here :
If thy ftill to their effence doth refine
So many drugs, is not the water thine?
Thefts thus become Juft Works ; they and their grace
Are wholly thine; thus doth the ftamp and face
Make that the King's that's ravifh'd from the mine ;
In others then 'tis oare, in thee 'tis coin.
 Bleft life of Authors unto whom we owe
Thofe that we have, and thofe that we want too;
Thou art all fo good that reading makes thee worfe,
And to have writ fo well's thine onely curfe ;
Secure then of thy merit, thou didft hate
That fervile bafe dependance upon Fate ;
Succefs thou ne'er thought'ft Vertue, nor that fit
Which Chance, or th' Ages Fafhion did make hit ;
Excluding thofe from life in after-time,
Who into Po'try firft brought luck and rime;
Who thought the Peoples breath good air, ftil'd name
What was but noife, and getting briefs for fame
Gather'd the many's fuffrages, and thence
Made commendations a benevolence:
Thy thoughts were thy own lawrell, and did win
That beft applaufe of being crown'd within.
And though th' exacting Age, when deeper years
Had interwoven fnow among thy heirs,
Would not permit thou fhouldft grow old, 'caufe they
Ne'er by their writing knew thee young ; we may
Say juftly, they're ungratefull, when they more
Condemn'd thee, 'caufe thou wert fo good before ; '
Thine art was thine acts blur, and they'l confefs
Thy ftrong perfumes made them not fmell thee lefs :
But, though to err with thee be no fmall fkill,
And we adore the laft draughts of thy quill;

Though

Though thofe thy thoughts, which the now queafie Age
Doth count but clods, and refufe of the Stage,
Will come up porcelane wit fome hundreds hence,
When there will be more manners and more fence;
'Twas judgement yet to yeeld, and we afford
Thy filence as much fame as once thy word :
Who like an aged oak, the leaves being gone,
Waft food before, and now religion ;
Thought ftill more rich, though not fo richly ftor'd,
View'd and enjoy'd before, but now ador'd.
   Great foul of numbers, whom we want and boaft,
Like curing gold, moft valu'd now thou 'rt loft ;
When we fhall feed on refufe offals, when
We fhall from corn to akorns turn agen ;
Then fhall we fee that thefe two names are one
Jonfon and *Poetry*, which now are gone.

Comed. Trag. Com. with other
Poems by W. Cartwright.
Lond. 1651. Ed.

F 4   Upon

Upon the Earle of Coventryes departure from us to the Angels.

SWEET Babe, whofe birth infpir'd me with a fong,
   And call'd my Mufe to trace thy dayes along;
Attending riper yeeres, with hope to finde
Such brave endeavours of thy noble minde,
As might deferve triumphant lines, and make
My fore-head bold a lawrell crowne to take :
How haft thou left us, and this earthly Stage,
(Not acting many months) in tender age?
Thou cam ft into this world a little Spie,
Where all things that could pleafe the eare and eye,
Were fet before thee, but thou found ft them toyes,
And flew'ft with fcornefull fmiles t' eternall joyes :
No vifage of Grim Death is fent t' affright
Thy fpotleffe foule, nor darkneffe blinds thy fight ;
But lightfome Angels with their golden wings
Ore-fpread thy cradle, and each fpirit brings
Some precious balme, for heav'nly phyficke meet,
To make the feparation foft and fweet.
The fparke infus'd by God departs away,
And bids the earthly weake companion ftay
With patience in that nurs'ry of the ground,
Where firft the feeds of Adam's limbes were found :

For

For time fhall come when thefe divided friends
Shall joyne againe, and know no feverall ends,
But change this fhort and momentary kiffe
To ftrict embraces of celeftiall bliffe.

> Bofworth-field and other Poems
> by Sir J. Beaumont—Ed. 1629.

On Lady Katherine Pafton, who died March 10, 1628.

CAN Man be filent and not praifes find,
  For her who lived the praife of woman-kind,
Whofe outward frame was lent the world to gefs,
What fhapes our fouls fhall wear in happinefs,
Whofe virtue did all ill fo overfwaye,
That her whole life was a communion daye.

> From the Church of Pafton,
> Norfolk.

On

On Eleanor Freeman, who died A. D. 1650,
aged 21.

A Virgin bloſſom in her May,
Of youth and virtues turn'd to clay;
Rich earth accompliſh'd with thoſe graces
That adorn Saints in heavenly places.
'Let not Death boaſt his conquering power
She'll riſe a Star, that fell a Flower.

From the Church of Tewkſbury,
Glouceſterſhire.

N EAR to this Eglantine
Encloſed lies the milke-white Armeline;
Once Chloris onlie joye,
Now only her annoy;
Who envied was of the moſt happy ſwaines,
That keepe their flockes on Mountaines, Dales, or Plaines:
For oft ſhe bore the wanton in her arme,
And oft her bed and boſom did him warme;
Now when unkindly fates did him deſtroy,
Bleſt dog he had the grace,
With tears for him that Chloris wet her face.

Drummond, p. 203. Ed. 8vo.

MISCELLA-

MISCELLANEOUS PIECES.

To the Queen, entertain'd at Night by the
Countefs of Anglefey.

FAIRE as unfhaded light ; or as the day
 In its firſt birth, when all the year was May ;
Sweet, as the Altars fmoak, or as the new
Unfolded bud, fwel'd by the early dew ;
Smooth, as the face of waters firſt appear'd,
Ere tides began to ſtrive, or winds were heard :
Kind as the willing Saints, and calmer farre,
Than in their ſleeps forgiven hermits are ;
You that are more, then our difcreter feare
Dares praife, with fuch full art, what make you here ?
Here, whére the Summer is fo little feen,
That leaves, (her cheapeſt wealth) fcarce reach at green.
You come, as if the filver Planet were
Miſled a while from her much-injur'd Sphere,
And t' eafe the travailes of her beames to-night,
In this fmall Lanthorn would contract her light.

The Works of Sir W. Davenant,
Lond. 1673. Fol. p. 218.

L O V E.

L O V E.

L OVE's fooner felt, then feen; his fubftance thinne
    Betwixt thofe fnowy mounts in ambufh lies:
Oft in the eyes he fpreads his fubtil ginne;
He therefore fooneft winnes that fafteft flies.
Fly thence, my dear, fly faft, my Thomalin:
Who him encounters once, for ever dies:
    But if he lurke between the ruddy lips,
    Unhappie foul, that thence his nectar fips,
While down into his heart the fugred poifon flips!

Oft in a voice he creeps down through the eare:
Oft from a blufhing cheek he lights his fire:
Oft fhrouds his golden flame in likeft hair:
Oft in a foft-fmooth fkin doth clofe retire:
Oft in a finile: oft in a filent teare:
And if all fail, yet Virtue's felf he'll hire:
    Himfelf's a dart, when nothing els can move.
    Who then the captive foul can well reprove,
When Love, and Vertue's felf become the darts of Love?

Pifcat. Eclog. by Ph. Fletche
Ecl. 6. St. 12, 13. Ed. 163

JEALOUS

JEALOUSY.

O Jealoufy! Daughter of Envy and Love,
  Moft wayward iffue of a gentle Sire ;
Fofter'd with fears, thy Father's joys t' improve ;
Mirth-marring Monfter, born a fubtle liar ;
Hateful unto thyfelf, flving thine owne defire ;
   Feeding upon Sufpect, that doth renew thee;
   Happy were Lovers if they never knew thee.

Thou haft a thoufand gates thou entereft by,
Condemning trembling Paffions to our heart:
Hundred-ey'd Argus, ever-waking fpy,
Pale hag, infernal fury, pleafure's fmart,
Envious obferver, prying in every part :
   Sufpicious, fearful, gazing ftill about thee ;
   O would to God that Love could be without thee !

Daniel's Compl. of Rofamond,
Ed. 1718, vol. I. p. 51.

A Vowe

A Vowe to Love faithfully howfoever he be rewarded.

SET me whereas the Sonne doth parch the grene,
  Or where his beames do not dyffolve the yfe,
In temperate heat, where he is felt, and fene,
In prefence preft of people, madde or wife;
Set me in hye, or yet in lowe degree,
In longeft night, or in the fhorteft day;
In cleareft fkye, or where cloudes thickeft be,
In lufty Youth, or when my haires are graye:
Set me in Heaven, in Earth, or elfe in Hell,
In hyll, or dale, or in the foaming flood;
Thrall, or at large, alyve wherefo I dwell,
Sicke, or in helthe, in evyll fame or good;
Hers will I be, and only with this thought,
Content myfelf, although my chance be nought.

Lord Surrey.

To

To A. L. Perſwaſions to LOVE.

STARVE not yourſelfe, becauſe you may
   Thereby make me pine away;
Nor let brittle beautie make
You your wiſer thoughts forſake:
For that lovely face will faile,
Beautie's ſweet, but beautie's fraile;
'Tis ſooner paſt, 'tis ſooner done
Then Summer's raine, or Winter's ſun:
Moſt fleeting when it is moſt deare,
'Tis gone while we but ſay 'tis here.
Theſe curious locks ſo aptly twin'd,
Whoſe every haire a ſoule doth bind,
Will change their auborn hue, and grow
White, and cold as Winter's ſnow.
That eye which now is Cupid's neſt
Will prove his grave, and all the reſt
Will follow; in the cheeke, chin, noſe,
Nor lilly ſhall be found nor roſe.
And what will then become of all
Thoſe, whom now you ſervants call?
Like ſwallowes when their ſummer's done,
They'le flye and ſeeke ſome warmer Sun.

> Poems by T. Carew, Eſquire.
> Lond. Ed. 1640.

HUE

HUE and CRY after CHLORIS.

I.

TELL me, ye wandring Spirits of the aire,
  Did you not fee a Nymph more bright, more faire
Than Beautie's darling, or of looks more fweet
Than ftolne content ? If fuch an one you meet,
Wait on her hourly wherefoere fhe flies,
And cry, and cry, Amyntor for abfence dies.

II.

Go fearch the vallies ; pluck up ev'ry rofe,
You'll find a fcente, a blufhe of her in thofe ;
Fifhe, fifh for pearle, or corall, there you'll fee
How oriental all her colours bee.
Go call the echoes to your aide, and cry,
Chloris, Chloris, for that's her name for whom I die.

III.

But ftay awhile, I have inform'd you ill,
Were fhe on Earth fhe had been with me ftill :
Go fly to Heav'n, examine ev'ry fphere,
And try what ftar hath lately lighted there ;
If any brighter than the fun you fee,
Fall down, fall down and worfhip it, for that is fhe.

Sele&t Ayres. Printed
for J. Playford, 1659.

LOVE's

L O V E's fervile Lot.

LOVE, miftreffe, is of many minds,
  Yet few know whom they ferve,
They reckon leaft how little Love
  Their fervice doth deferve.

The will fhe robbeth from the wit
  The fenfe from reafon's lore,
She is delightfull in the rine,
  Corrupted in the core.

She fhroudeth vice in vertue's vaile,
  Pretending good in ill,
She offereth joy, affordeth griefe,
  A kiffe where fhe doth kill.

A honey-fhower raines from her lips,
  Sweet lights fhine in her face,
She hath the blufh of virgine mind,
  The mind of vipers race.

She makes thee feeke, yet feare to find ;
  To finde, but not enjoy :
In many frownes fome gliding fmiles
  Shee yeelds to more annoy.

Shee wooes thee to come neere her fire,
   Yet doth fhe draw it from thee,
Farre off fhe makes thy hart to fry,
   And yet to freeze within thee.

She letteth fall fome luring baits
   For fooles to gather up ;
Too fweete, too fowre, to everie tafte
   She tempereth her cup.

Soft foules fhe binds in tender twift,
   Small flyes in fpinners webbe ;
She fets afloate fome luring ftreames
   But makes them foone to ebbe.

Her watrie eyes have burning force ;
   Her floods and flames confpire :
Tears kindle fparks, fobs fuell are,
   And fighs doe blow her fire.

May never was the Month of Love,
   For May is full of flowers ;
But rather Aprill, wet by kind,
   For Love is full of fhowers.

Like Tyrant, cruel wound fhe gives,
   Like Surgeon, falve fhe lends ;
But falve and fore have equall force,
   For death is both their ends.

With foothing words, inthralled foules
   She chaines in fervile bands ;
Her eye in filence has a fpeach
   Which eye beft underftands.

Her little fweet hath many fowres,
   Short hap`immortal harmes ;
Her loving lookes are murd'ring darts,
   Her fongs bewitching charmes.

Like Winter rofe and Summer ife
   Her joyes are ftill untimely ;
Before her Hope, behind Remorfe :
   Faire firft, in fine unfeemely.

Moodes, paffions, fancies, jealous fits,
   Attend upon her traine :
She yeeldeth reft without repofe,
   And Heaven in hellifh paine.

Her houfe is Sloth, her doore Deceite,
   And flipperie Hope her ftaires ;
Unbafhfull Boldnefs bids her guefts,
   And every Vice repaires.

Her dyet is of fuch delights
   As pleafe till they be paft ;
But then the poyfon kills the hart,
   That did entife the tafte.

Her fleepe in Sinne doth end in Wrath,
   Remorfe rings her awake ;
Death cals her up, Shame drives her out,
   Defpaires her up-fhot make.

Plow not the feas, fowe not the fands,
   Leave off your idle paine ;
Seeke other miftreffe for your mindes,
   Love's fervice is in vaine.

ROBERT SOUTHWELL.

G 2   DESCRIP-

DESCRIPTION of SPRING,

Wherein eche thing renewes, fave only the Lover.

THE foote Seafon that bud and bloome fourth bringes,
   With grene hath cladde the hyll, and eke the vale,
The Nightingall with feathers new fhe finges ;
The turtle to her mate hath told her tale :
Somer is come, for every fpray now fpringes ;
The hart hath hong hys olde hed on the pale,
The bucke in brake his winter coate he flynges :
The fifhes flete with new repayred fcale ;
The adder all her flough away fhe flynges ;
The fwift fwalow purfueth the flyes fmale,
The bufy bee her hony now fhe mynges ;
Winter is worne that was the floures bale ;
And thus I fce among thefe pleafant thynges
Eche care decayes, and yet my forrow fprynges.

Lord SURREY.

VERSES

VERSES by QUEEN ELIZABETH.

I Greeve and dare not fhewe my difcontent,
  I love and yet am forft to feeme to hate,
I doe yet dare not fay I ever meant,
I feeme ftarke mute, but inwardly doe prate
    I am and not, I freeze and yet am burn'd
    Since from myfelf, my other felfe I turn'd.

My care is like my fhaddowe in the fune
Followes me fliinge, flies when I purfue it,
Standes and lies by me, does what I have done,
This too familiar care does make me rue it,
    No meanes I finde to rid him from my breft,
    Till by the end of thinges it be fuppreft.

Some gentler paffions flide into my minde,
For I am fofte and made of meltinge fnowe ;
Or be more cruell, Love, and fo be kynd,
Let mee or flote or finke, be high or lowe,
    Or let me live with fome more fweete content,
    Or dye and foe forget what love ere meant.

Signed, " *Finis, Eliza. Regina,* upon
Mount Zeurs departure," Afhmol.
Muf. MSS. 6969. (781) p. 142.

To Mrs. E. B. upon a fudden Surprifal.

A PELLES, prince of Painters, did
    All others in that art exceed :
But you furpafs him, for he took
    Some pains and time to draw a look,
You, in a trice and moment's fpace,
    Have pourtray'd in my heart your face.

Poems by J. Howell.
1664, Lond. Ed.

On FRIENDSHIP.

N O T ftayed ftate, but feeble ftay,
    Not coftly robes, but bare array ;
Not paffed welth, but prefent want.
Not heped ftore, but fclender fkant,
Not plenties purfe, but poore eftate,
Not happy hap, but froward fate ;
Not wifh at wil, but want of joy,
Not harts good helth, but harts annoy :

Not

Not freedomes ufe, but prifoners thrall,
Not coftly feate, but loweft fall:
Not weale I meane, but wretched wo,
Doth truely try, the freend from foe:
And nowght but frowarde Fortune proves,
Who fauning faines, or fimply loves.

Paradife of Dęynty Devife.
Fol. 1, 3. figned M. Yloop.

An APOSTROPHE to CHARITY.

WHERE is this love become in later age?
    Alas! 'tis gone in endleffe pilgrimage
From hence, and never to returne, I doubt,
Till revolution wheele thofe times about;
Chill brefts have ftarv'd her here, and fhe is driven
Away; and with Aftræa fled to Heaven.
Poore Charity, that naked Babe, is gone,
Her honey's fpent, and all her ftore is done;
Her wingleffe bees can finde out ne're a bloome,
And crooked Até doth ufurpe her roome;
Nepenthe's dry, and Love can get no drinke,
And curs'd Ardenne flowes above the brinke.

A Feaſt for Wormes. Med. 5.
1650. Lond. by F. Quarles,

To CHASTITY,

O Chaſtity, the flower of the ſoule,
How is thy perfeét fairneſſe turn'd to foule!
How are thy bloſſomes blaſted all to duſt,
By ſudden lightning of untamed luſt!
How haſt thou thus defil'd thy iv'ry feet!
Thy ſweetneſſé that was once, how 'far from ſweet!
Where are thy maiden ſmiles, thy bluſhing cheek?
Thy lamb-like countenance, ſo faire, ſo meeke?
Where is that ſpotleſſe Flower that while-ere
Within thy liiy-boſome thou didſt weare?
Has wanton Cupid ſnatcht it, hath his dart
Sent courtly tokens to thy ſimple heart?
Where doſt thou bide? the Country halfe diſclaimes thee,
The City wonders when a body names thee:
Or have the rurall woods ingroſt thee there,
And thus foreſtall'd our empty markets here?
Sure thou art not, or kept where no man ſhowes thee
Or chang'd ſo much, ſcarce man or woman knowes thee.

Hiſt. of Queen Eſter,
by F. Quarles.

To his Sonne VINCENT CORBET.

WHAT I ſhall leave thee none can tell,
    But all ſhall ſay I wiſh thee well :
I wiſh thee *(Vin)* before all wealth,
Both bodily and ghoſtly health ;
Nor too much wealth, nor wit come to thee,
So much of either may undoe thee.
I wiſh thee learning, not for ſhow,
Enough for to inſtruct, and know ;
Not ſuch as gentlemen require
To prate at table, or at fire.
I wiſh thee all thy mother's graces,
Thy father's fortunes, and his places.
I wiſh thee friends, and one at Court
Not to build on but ſupport ;
To keepe thee, not in doing many
Oppreſſions, but from ſuffering any.
I wiſh thee peace in all thy wayes,
Nor lazy nor contentious dayes ;
And when thy ſoule and body part,
As innocent as now thou art.

Certain Elegant Poems, Written
by Dr. Corbet, &c. Lond. 1647.

The SURRENDER.

M Y once dear Love, haplefs that I no more
   Muft call thee fo ; the rich affections ftore
That fed our hopes, lies now exhauft and fpent,
Like fummes of treafure unto bankrupts lent.
We that did nothing ftudy but the way
To love each other, with which thoughts the day
Rofe with delight to us, and with them fet,
Muft learn the hateful art how to forget.
We that did nothing wifh that Heav'n could give
Beyond ourfelves, nor did defire to live
Beyond that wifh, all thefe now cancell muft
As if not writ in faith, but words and duft.
Yet witnefs thofe cleer vowes which Lovers make,
Witnefs the chaft defires that never brake
Into unruly hearts ; witnefs that breft
Which in thy bofom anchor'd his whole reft,
'Tis no default in us, I dare acquite
Thy maiden faith, thy purpofe fair and white
As thy pure felf, crofs Planets did envie
Us to each other, and Heaven did untie
Fafter then vowes could binde.   O that the Starres
When Lovers meet, fhould ftand oppos'd in warres !
Since then fome higher Deftinies command,
Let us not ftrive nor labour to withftand

Vhat is paft help, the longeft date of grief
)an never yield a hope of our relief;
\nd though we wafte ourfelves in moift laments,
Tears may drown us, but not our difcontents.
'old back our arms, take home our fruitlefs loves
Fhat muft new fortunes trie, like Turtle Doves
)iflodged from their haunts, we muft in tears
Jnwind a love knit up in many years.
In this laft kifs I here furrender thee
Back to thyfelf, fo thou againe art free.
Thou in an other, fad as that, refend
The trueft heart that lover ere did lend.
Now turn from each, fo fare our fever'd hearts
As the divorc't foul from her body parts.

Dr. King's Poems,

p. 24.

The LEGACY,

MY deareft Love! when thou and I muft part
And th' icy hand of Death fhall feize that heart
Which is all thine; within fome fpacious will
I'le leave no blanks for legacies to fill :
'Tis my ambition to dye one of thofe
Who but himfelf hath nothing to difpofe.
And fince that is already thine, what need
I to re-give it by fome newer deed ?
Yet take it once again, free circumftance
Does oft the value of mean things advance;

Whe

Who thus repeats what he bequeath'd before,
Proclaims his bounty richer then his ftore.
But let me not upon my Love beftow
What is not worth the giving.   I do ow
Somewhat to duft: my bodies pamper'd care
Hungry corruption and the worm will fhare.
That moul'dring relick which in earth muft lie
Would prove a gift of horrour to thine eie
With this caft ragge of my mortalitie
Let all my faults and errours buried be.
And as thy fear-cloth rots, fo may kind fate
Thofe worft acts of my life incinerate.
He fhall in ftory fill a glorious room
Whofe afhes and whofe fins fleep in one tomb.
If now to my cold hearfe thou deign to bring
Some melting fighs as thy laft offering,
My peacefull exequies are crown'd, nor fhall
I afk more honour at my Funerall.
Thou wilt more richly 'balm me with thy tears
Then all the nard fragrant Arabia bears.
And as the Paphian Queen by her griefs fhow'r
Brought up her dead Love's Spirit in a flow'r:
So by thofe precious drops rain'd from thine eies,
Out of my duft, O may fome Vertue rife !
And like thy better Genius thee attend,
Till thou in my dark period fhalt end.
Laftly, my conftant truth let me commend
To him thou choofeft next to be thy friend.
For (witnefs all things good) I would not have
Thy Youth and Beauty married to my grave,
'Twould fhew thou didft repent the ftyle of wife
Should'ft thou relapfe into a fingle life.
They with prepofterous grief the world delude
Who mourn for their loft mates in folitude ;

Since Widdow-hood more ſtrongly doth enforce
The much-lamented lot of their divorce.
Themſelves then of their loſſes guilty are
Who may, yet will not ſuffer a repaire.
Thoſe were Barbarian wives that did invent
Weeping to death at th' Huſband's monument,
But in more civil Rites ſhe doth approve
Her firſt, who ventures on a ſecond Love;
For elſe it may be thought if ſhe refrain,
She ſped ſo ill ſhe durſt not trie again,
Up then my Love, and chooſe ſome worthier one
Who may ſupply my room when I am gone;
So will the ſtock of our affection thrive
No leſs in death, then were I ſtill alive.
And in my urne l ſhall rejoyce, that I
Am both Teſtatour thus and legacie.

Dr. King's Poems,
p. 28.

The PRIMROSE.

A SKE me why I fend you here,
   This firftling of the infant yeare ;
Afke me why I fend to you,
This primrofe all bepearl'd with dew ;
I ftrait will whifper in Your eares,
The fweets of Love are wafh't with teares.

Afke me why this flower doth fhew
So yellow, greene, and fickly too ;
Afke me why the ftalke is weake,
And bending yet it doth not breake;
I muft tell you thefe difcover,
What doubts and feares are in a Lover.

Poems by T. Carew Efquire.
Lond. 1640.

A CAUTION

A CAUTION for COURTLY DAMSELS.

BEWARE, fair Maid, of mighty Courtiers oaths,
　Take heed what gifts or favours you receive ;
Let not the fading gloffe of filken cloaths
Dazzle your vertues, or your fame bereave:
　　For once but leave the hold you have of Grace,
　　Who will regard your fortune or your face ?

Each greedy hand will ftrive to catch the flower,
When none regard the ftalke it growes upon ;
Bafeneffe defires the fruit ftill to devoure,
And leave the tree to fall or ftand alone:
　　But this advife, fair Creature, take of mee,
　　Let none take fruit unleffe hee'll have the tree.

Beleeve not oaths, nor much-protefting men,
Credit no vowes, nor a bewailing fong;
Let Courtiers fweare, forfweare, and fweare agen,
The heart doth live ten regions from the tongue:
　　For when with oaths and vows they make you tremble,
　　Beleeve them leaft for then they moft diffemble.

Beware

Beware left Cœrfus doe corrupt thy minde,
Or fond Ambition fell thy modefty;
Say, though a King thou even courteous finde,
Hee cannot pardon thy impurity.
    Begin with Kings, to fubjects you will fall,
    From Lord to Lackey, and at laft to all.

              See Epigrams fubjoin'd to J. Sylvefter's
              Du Bartas. 1641. Lond.

The Frailtye and hurtfulnes of Beautie.

BRITTLE Beautie that Nature made fo fraile,
    Whereof the gifte is fmal, and fhort the Seafon;
Flowring to-day, to-morrowe apt to faile,
'Tickled treafure, abhorred of 'reafon:
Dangerous to deale with, vaine, of none availe,
Coftly in keeping, paft, not worthe two peafon;
Slipper in fliding, as is an Eles taile;
Harde to attain, once gotten not geafon.
Jewell of jeopardie, that peril doth affaile,
Falfe and untrewe, enticed oft to treafon;
Enemy to Youth, that moft may I bewaile;
Ah bitter fwete! infecting as the poyfon,
Thou fareft as frute, that with the froft is taken,
To-day redy ripe, to-morrow al to fhaken

                      Lord SURREY.

                             To

TO THE ROSE.

SWEET Rose, whence is this hue
     Which does all hues excell ?
Whence this moſt fragrant ſmell ?
And whence this form and gracing grace in you ?
In flow'ry Pœſtum's fields perhaps you grew,
Or Hybla's hills you bred,
Or odoriferous Enna's plains you fed,
Or Tmolus, or where boar young Adon ſlew ;
Or hath the Queen of Love you dy'd of new
In that dear blood, which makes you look ſo red ?
        No, none of theſe, but cauſe more high you bliſt ;
        My Lady's breaſt you bore, her lips you kiſt.
                    Drummond's Son, and Madrig,
                    Edinb. Ed. 1711. Fol.

DRY thoſe fair, thoſe chryſtal eyes
     Which like growing fountains riſe
To drown their banks.   Griefs ſullen brooks
Would better flow in furrow'd looks.
Thy lovely face was never meant
To be the ſhoar of diſcontent.

Then clear thofe wat'rifh ftarres again,
Which elfe portend a lafting rain ;
Left the clouds which fettle there
Prolong my Winter all the Year:
And the example others make
In love with Sorrow for thy fake.

Dr. King's Poems.
p. 19.

LESBIA ON HER SPARROW.

TELL me not of joy: there's none
   Now my little Sparrow's gone ;
     He, juft as you,
     Would toy and wooe,
He would chirp and flatter me,
He would hang the wing awhile,
'Till at length he faw me fmile,
Lord how fullen he would be ?

He would catch a crumb, and then
Sporting let it goe agen,
     He from my lip
     Would moyfture fip.
He would from my trencher feed,
Then would hop, and then would run,
And cry *Philip* when h' had done,
O whofe heart can choofe but bleed ?

O how

O how eager would he fight,
And'ne'r hurt though he did bite:
 No morn did pafs
 But on my glafs
He would fit, and mark, and do
What I did, now ruffle all
His feathers o'r, now let 'em fall
And then ftraightway fleek them too.

Whence will Cupid get his darts
Feather'd now to pierce our hearts;
 A wound he may,
 Not Love conveigh,
Now this faithfull Bird is gone,
O let mournfull Turtles joyn
With loving Red-breafts, and combine
To fing Dirges o'er his ftone.

Com. Trag. Com. with other
Poems, by Mr. W. Cartwright.
Lond. 1651.

    MADRIGAL

M A D R I G A L.

M Y Thoughts hold mortal ſtrife,
　　I do deteſt my life,
And with lamenting cries
Peace to my ſoul to bring,
Oft call that Prince, which here doth monarchize,
But he grim grinning King,
Who catives ſcorns, and doth the bleſt ſurpriſe
　　Late having deckt with Beauty's Roſe his tomb,
　　Diſdains to crop a weed, and will not come.

Drummond. Edinb. 1711. Fol. Ed.

SONNETS.

S O N N E T S.

To Sir WILLIAM ALEXANDER.

THO' I have twice been at the doors of Death,
And twice found fhut thofe gates which ever mourn ;
This but a lightning is : truce ta'en to breath
For late-born forrowes augure fleet return.
Amid thy facred cares, and courtly toils,
Alexis. when thou fhalt hear wand'ring Fame
Tell, Death hath triumph'd o'er my mortal fpoils,
And that on Earth I am but a fad name :
If thou e'er held me dear, by all our love,
By all that blifs, thofe joys, Heaven here us gave ;
I conjure thee, and by the Maids of Jove,
To 'grave this fhort remembrance on my grave ;
" Here Damon lies, whofe fongs did fometime grace
" The murmuring Efk—may rofes fhade the place."

Drummond.

To

To D E L I A.

L OO K Delia, how w' eſteem the half-blown roſe,
The image of thy bluſh, and Summer's honour !
Whilſt yet her tender bud doth undiſcloſe
That full of Beauty, Time beſtowes upon her.
No ſooner ſpreads her glory in the air,
But ſtrait her wide-blown pomp comes to decline ;
She then is ſcorn'd, that late adorn'd the Fair ;
So fade the roſes of thoſe cheeks of thine !
No April can revive thy wither'd flow'rs,
Whoſe ſpringing grace adorns thy glory now :
Swift ſpeedy Time, feather'd with flying hours,
Diſſolves the beauty of the faireſt brow,
Then do not thou ſuch treaſure waſte in vain
But love now, whilſt thou may'ſt be lov'd again.

Daniel XXXVI. Son.

A Viſion

A Viſion upon this conçeit of the Fairy Queen.

METHOUGHT I ſaw the Grave where Laura lay,
　　Within that Temple where the Veſtal Flame
Was wont to burn ; and paſſing by that way,
To ſee that buryed duſt of living fame
Whoſe tomb fair Love, and fairer Vertue kept,
All ſuddenly I ſaw the Fairy Queen :
At whoſe approach, the Soul of Petrarch wept,
And from thenceforth thoſe Graces were not ſeen.
For they this Queen attended ; in whoſe ſteed
Oblivion laid him down on Laura's herſe :
Hereat the hardeſt ſtones were ſeen to bleed,
And grones of buried Ghoſts the Heavens did perſe.
　　Where Homer's Spright did tremble all for grief
　　And curſt th' acceſs of that celeſtial Thief.

　　　　　　　　　　　　Sir W. Raleigh.

　　　　　　　　To

To S L E E P.

S L E E P, Silence Child, fweet Father of foft reft,
  Prince whofe approach peace to all mortalls brings,
Indifferent Hoft to fhepheards and to kings,
Sole comforter of minds with griefe oppreft.
Loe, by thy charming rod all breathing things
Lie flumbring, with forgetfulneffe poffeft,
And yet o'er me to fpread thy drowfie wings
Thou fpares (alas) who cannot be thy gueft.
Since I am thine, O come, but with that face
To inward light which thou art wont to fhow,
With fained folace eafe a true-felt woe,
Or if, deafe God, thou doe denie that grace,
    Come as thou wilt, and what thou wilt bequeath,
    I long to kiffe the image of my death.

                   Drummond, Edinb. 1616.

To the RIVER ANKOR.

CLEAR Ankor, on whofe filver-fanded fhore,
   My foul-fhrin'd Saint, my fair Idea lies,
O bleffed Brook, whofe milk-white fwans adore
Thy cryftal ftream refined by her eyes,
Where fweet myrrh-breathing Zephyr in the Spring
Gently diftills his nectar-dropping fhowers,
Where nightingales in Arden fit and fing
Amongft the dainty dew-impearled flowers ;
Say thus, fair Brook, when thou fhalt fee thy Queen,
Lo, here thy Shepherd fpent his wand'ring years ;
And in thefe fhades, dear Nymph, he oft had been,
And here to thee he facrific'd his tears :
      Fair Arden, thou my Tempe art alone,
      And thou, Sweet Ankor, art my Helicon.

                                        Drayton, LIII. Son.

                                                      I know

I Know that all beneath the Moone decayes,
And what by mortalles in this world is brought,
In Time's great periods shall returne to nought,
That faireſt ſtates have fatall nights and dayes:
I know how all the Muſes heavenly layes;
With toyle of ſpright which are ſo dearly bought,
As idle ſounds, of few, or none are ſought,
And that nought lighter is than airie praiſe.
I know fraile Beautie like the purple flowre,
To which one morne of birth and death affords,
That Love a jarring is of mindes accords,
Where Senſe and Will invaſſall Reaſon's power:
    Know what I liſt, this all can not mee move
    But that (oh mee!) I both muſt write and love.
               Drummond, Edinb. 1616.

R ESTORE thy Treſſes to the golden Oar;
Yield Citherea's Son thoſe Arks of Love:
Bequeath the Heav'ns the Stars that I adore;
And to th' Orient do thy Pearls remove.
Yield thy hands pride unto the ivory white;
T' Arabian Odors give thy breathing ſweet:
Reſtore thy Bluſh unto Aurora bright;
To Thetis give the honour of thy Feet.

                                    Let

Let Venus have thy Graces her refign'd ;
And thy fweet Voice give back unto the Spheres :
But yet reftore thy fierce and cruel Mind
To Hyrcan Tygers, and to ruthlefs Bears.
  Yield to the Marble thy hard Heart again ;
  So fhalt thou ceafe to plague, and I to pain.

Daniel, XIX. Son.
1718. Ed. 2 V.

SINCE there's no help, come let us kifs and part,
 Nay, I have done, you get no more of me,
And I am glad, yea glad with all my heart,
That thus fo cleanly I myfelf can free,
Shake hands for ever, cancel all our vows,
And when we meet at any time again,
Be it not feen in either of our brows,
That we one jot of former love retain ;
Now at the laft gafp of Love's lateft breath,
When his pulfe failing, paffion fpeechlefs lies,
When Faith is kneeling by his bed of death,
And Innocence is clofing up his eyes,
  Now if thou would'ft, when all have given him over
  From death to life thou might'ft him yet recover.

Dayton, LXI. Son.

To

To his L U T E,

M Y Lute, bee as thou waft, when thou didft grow
With thy greene mother in fome fhadie grove,
When immelodious windes but made thee move,
And birds on thee their ramage did beftow.
Sith that deare voyce, which did thy founds approve
Which ufed in fuch harmonious ftraines to flow,
Is reft from Earth to tune thofe fpheares above,
What art thou but a harbinger of woe?
Thy pleafing notes be pleafing notes no more,
But orphane wailings to the fainting eare,
Each ftoppe a figh, each found drawes foorth a teare,
Be therefore filent as in woods before,
    Or if that any hand to touch thee daigne,
    Like widow'd Turtle ftill her loffe complaine.

Drummond, Edin. Ed. 1616.

To

To S L E E P.

CARE-charmer Sleep, Son of the fable Night;
  Brother to Death, in filent darknefs born :
Relieve my languifh, and reftore the light ;
With dark forgetting of my care, return.
And let the day be time enough to mourn
The Shipwreck of my ill-advifed Youth :
Let waking eyes fuffice to wail their fcorn,
Without the torments of the night's untruth.
Ceafe, dreams, the images of day-defires,
To model forth the paffions of the morrow ;
Never let rifing Sun approve you liars,
To add more grief to aggravate my forrow.
    Still let me fleep, embracing clouds in vain ;
    And never wake to feel the day's difdain.

Daniel, XLI. Son.

MY heart was flain, and none but you and I;
Who fhould I think the murder fhould commit?
Since but yourfelf there was no creature by,
But only I; guiltlefs of murd'ring it.
It flew itfelf; the verdict on the view
Do quit the dead, and me not acceffary:
Well, well, I fear it will be prov'd by you,
The evidence fo great a proof doth carry.
But O, fee, fee, we need enquire no further,
Upon your lips the fcarlet drops are found,
And in your eye the Boy that did the murder,
Your cheeks yet pale, fince firft he gave the wound.
    By this I fee, however things be paft,
    Yet Heaven will ftill have murder out at laft.

Drayton, II. Son.

ALEXIS, here fhee ftay'd, among thefe pines
(Sweet Hermitreffe) fhee did alone repaire,
Here did fhe fpreade the treafure of her haire,
More rich than that brought from the Cholchian mines.
She fet her by thefe mufket Eglantines;
The happie place the print feemes yet to beare,
Her voyce did fweeten here thy fugred lines,
To which windes, trees, beafts, birds, did lend their eare;
Mee

Mee here fhe firft perceiv'd, and here a morne
Of bright carnations did orefpreade her face,
Here did fhee figh, there firft my hopes were borne,
And I firft got a pledge of promis'd grace :
　　But ah ! what ferv'd it to be happie fo?
　　Sith paffed pleafures double but new woe.

　　　　　　　　　　　　　　　Drummond.

UNTO the boundlefs Ocean of thy Beauty,
　　Runs this poor River, charg'd with ftreams of zea
Returning thee the tribute of my duty,
Which here my Love, my Youth, my Plaints reveal.
Here I unclafp the Book of my charg'd foul,
Where I have caft th' Accounts of all my care :
Here have I fumm'd my fighs ; here I enroll
How they were fpent for thee ; look what they are,
Look on the dear expences of my Youth,
And fee how juft I reckon with thine eyes :
Examine well thy beauty with my truth ;
And crofs my cares, ere greater fums arife.
　　Read it, fweet Maid, tho' it be done but flightly;
　　Who can fhew all his Love, doth love but lightly.

　　　　　　　　　　　　　　Daniel, I. Son.

Truft

TRUST not, fweet Soule, thofe curled waves of gold
   With gentle tides which on your temples flow,
Nor temples fpread with flackes of virgine fnow,
Nor fnow of cheekes with Tyrian graine enroll'd.
Trust not thofe fhining lights which wrought my woe,
When firft I did their burning rayes beholde,
Nor voyce, whofe founds more ftrange effects doe fhow
Than of the Thracian Harper have beene tolde :
Looke to this dying Lille, fading Rofe,
Darke Hyacinthe, of late whofe blufhing beames
Made all the neighbouring herbes and graffe rejoyce,
And thinke how little is twixt Life's extreames :
   The cruell Tyrant that did kill thofe flow'rs,
   Shall once (aye mee!) not fpare that Spring of yours.

                          Drummond, Edinb. 1616.

LOVE banifh'd Heaven, in Earth was held in fcorn,
   Wand'ring abroad in need and beggary ;
And wanting friends, tho' of a Goddefs born,
Yet crav'd the alms of fuch as paffed by :
I, like a man devout and charitable,
Cloathed the naked, lodg'd this wand'ring gueft,
With fighs and teares ftill furnifhing his table,
With what might make the miferable bleft :

But this Ungrateful, for my good defert,
Intic'd my thoughts againſt me to conſpire,
Who gave conſent to ſteal away my heart,
And ſet my breaſt, his lodging on a fire,
    Well, well, my friends, when beggars grow thus bold,
    No marvel then tho' charity grow cold.

Drayton, XXIII. Son.

W H A T doth it ſerve to ſee Sunnes burning face?
    And ſkies enamell'd with both Indies gold?
Or moone at night in jettie chariot roll'd?
And all the glorie of that ſtarrie place?
What doth it ſerve Earth's beautie to behold?
The mountaines pride, the meadowes flowrie grace;
The ſtatelie comelineſſe of forreſts old,
The ſport of flowds which would themſelves embrace?
What doth it ſerve to heare the Sylvans ſongs,
The wanton Mearle, the Nightingalle's ſad ſtraines,
Which in darke ſhades ſeeme to deplore my wrongs?
For what doth ſerve all that this world containes,
    Sith Shee for whom thoſe once to mee were deare,
    No part of them can have now with mee heare.

Drummond.

WHY fhould I fing in verfe, why fhould I frame
      Thefe fad neglected notes for her dear fake ?
Why fhould I offer up unto her name,
The fweeteft facrifice my youth can make ?
Why fhould I ftrive to make her live for ever,
That never deigns to give me joy to live ?
Why fhould my afflicted mufe fo much endeavour
Such honour unto cruelty to give ?
If her defects have purchas'd her this fame,
What fhould her virtues do, her fmiles, her love ?
If this her worft, how fhould her beft inflame ?
What paffions would her milder favours move ?
      Favours, I think, would fenfe quite overcome,
      And that makes happy Lovers ever dumb.

                              Daniel, XVII. Son.

IF croft with all mifhaps be my poor Life,
   If one fhort day I never fpent in mirth,
If my fpirit with itfelf holds lafting ftrife,
If Sorrowes death is but new Sorrowes birth?
If this vaine World bee but a fable ftage
Where flave-born Man playes to the fcoffing ftarres,
If Youth be tofs'd with Love, with Weakneffe Age,
If Knowledge ferve to hold our thoughts in warres ?

                                              If.

If tlme can clofe the hundred mouths of Fame,
And make what's long fince paft, like that to bee,
If Vertue only bee an idle name,
If I when 1 was borne was borne to die?
    Why feeke I to prolong thefe loathfome dayes,
    The faireft rofe in fhorteft time decayes.

                             Drummond.

To the SPRING.

S W E E T Spring, thou turn'ft with all thy goodlie traine,
  Thy head with flames, thy mantle bright with flow'rs,
The Zephyres curle the greene lockes of the plaine,
The cloudes for joy in pearles weepe down their fhow'rs,
Thou turn'ft (fweet Youth) but ah my pleafant howres,
And happie dayes with thee come not againe,
The fad memorialls only of my paine
Doe with thee turne, which turne my fweets in fow'rs.
Thou art the fame which ftill thou was before,
Delicious, wanton, amiable, faire,
But fhee, whofe breath embaulmed thy wholefome aire,
Is gone : nor gold nor gemmes her can reftore.
    Neglected Vertue, Seafons goe and come
    While thine forgot lie clofed in a Tombe.

                             Drummond.

L OOK E how the flowre, which lingringlie doth fade,
  The Morning's Darling late, the Summer's Queene,
Spoyl'd of that juice, which kept it freſh and greene,
As high as it did raiſe, bowes low the head ;
Right ſo my Life (Contentments being dead,
Or in their contraries but onelie ſeene)
With ſwifter ſpeede declines than earſt it ſpred,
And (blaſted) ſcarce now ſhowes what it hath beene.
As doth the Pilgrime therefore whom the night
By darkneſſe would impriſon on his way,
Thinke on thy Home, (my Soule) and thinke aright,
Of what yet reſtes thee of Life's waſting day :
  Thy Sunne poſtes weſtward, paſſed is thy morne,
  And twice it is not given thee to be born.

Drummond, Flowres of Sion:
Ed. 1630, 4to.

T •

To the NIGHTINGALE.

S WE E T Bird, that fing'ft awoy the early howres,
    Of winters palt, or comming void of care,
Well pleafed with delights which prefent are,
Faire Seafones, budding fprayes, fweet-fmelling flowres:
To rocks, to fprings, to rils, from leavie bowres
Thou thy Creator's goodneffe doft declare,
And what deare gifts on thee hee did not fpare,
A ftaine to humane fence in fin that lowres.
What Soule can be fo ficke, which by thy fongs
(Attir'd in fweetneffe) fweetly is not driven
Quite to forget Earth's turmoiles, fpights and wrongs,
And lift a reverend eye and thought to Heaven?
    Sweet artleffe Songftarre, thou my minde doft raife
    To ayres of Spheares, yes, and to Angels layes.

Drummond's Flowers cf Sion.

S P E E C H E S,

Harold's fpeech before the Battle of Haftings.

" SEE valiant War-friends yonder be the firft, the laft,
  and all
The agents of our Enemies, they hencefoorth cannot call
Supplies; for weedes at *Normandie* by this in Porches groe:
Then conquer thefe would conquer you, and dread no further
  foe.
They are no ftouter than the Brutes, whom we did hence
  exile :
Nor ftronger than the fturdy Danes, our victory ere while :
Not Saxonie could once containe, or fcarce the world befide
Our fathers, who did fway by fword where lifted them to bide:
Then doe not yee degenerate, take courage by difcent,
And by their burialles, not abode, their force and flight pre-
  vent.
Yee have in hand your Countries caufe, a conqueft they pre-
  tend,
Which (were yee not the fame yee be) even cowards would de-
  fend.

                                      I graunt

I graunt that part of us are fled and linked to the foe,
And glad I am our Armie is of traytours cleered fo :
Yea pardon hath he to depart that ſtayeth mal-content :
I priſe the mind above the man, like zeale hath like event.
Yeat truth it is, no well or ill this Iſland ever had,
But through the well or ill ſupport of ſubjects good or bad :
Not Cæſar, Hengeſt, Swayn, or now (which neretheles ſhall
    fayle)
The Normane Baſtard, Albion true, did, could, or can pre-
    vayle.
But to be ſelfe-falſe in this Iſle a ſelfe-foe ever is,
Yeat wot I, never traytour did his treaſons ſtipend mis.
Shrinke who will ſhrinke, let armors wayte preſſe downe the
    burd'ned earth,
My foes, with wondring eyes ſhall fee I over-prize my death.
But ſince ye all (for all, I hope, alike affected bee,
Your wives, your children, lives, and land, from ſervitude to
    free)
Are armed both in ſhew and zeale, then glorioufly contend,
To winne and weare the home-brought ſpoyles, of Victorie
    the end.
Let not the Skinners daughter Sonne poſſeſſe what he pre-
    tends,
He lives to die a noble death that life for freedome ſpends."

Duke W I L L I A M's Speech.

"TO live upon or lie within this is my ground or grave
(My loving Souldiers), one of twaine your Duke refolves
    to have.
Nor be ye *Normanes* now to feeke in what you fhould be ftout,
Ye come amidft the Englifh pikes to hewe your honors out,
Ye come to winne the fame by launce, that is your owne by
    law,
Ye come, I fay, in righteous warre revenging fwords to draw.
Howbeit of more hardie foes no paffed flight hath fpead ⌉
    yee,   ⎬
Since Rollo to your now-abode with bands victorious lead
    yee,   ⎬
Or Turchus, Sonne of Troylus, in Scythian Fazo bread
    yee. ⌋
Then worthy your progenitors yee Seede of Pryam's fonne
Exployt this Buifneffe, Rollons do that which yee wifh be
    done.
Three people have as many times got and forgone this fhore,
It refteth now yee conquer it not to be conquered more:
For Normane and the Saxon blood conjoyning, as it may,
From that conforted feede the Crowne fhall never paffe away,
Before us are our armed foes, behind us are the feas,
On either fide the foe hath holdes of fuccour and for eafe :
But that advantage fhall returne their difadvantage thus,
If ye obferve no fhore is left the which may fhelter us,
And fo hold out amidft the rough whil'ft they hale in for lee,
Whereas, whil'ft men fecurely fayle, not feldome fhipwracks
    bee,

                                   What

I graunt that part of us are fled and linked to the foe,
And glad I am our Armie is of traytours cleered fo :
Yea pardon hath he to depart that ftayeth mal-content :
I prife the mind above the man, like zeale hath like event.
Yeat truth it is, no well or ill this Ifland ever had,
But through the well or ill fupport of fubjects good or bad :
Not Cæfar, Hengeft, Swayn, or now (which neretheles fhall
    fayle)
The Normane Baftard, Albion true, did, could, or can pre-
    vayle.
But to be felfe-falfe in this Ifle a felfe-foe ever is,
Yeat wot I, never traytour did his treafons ftipend mis.
Shrinke who will fhrinke, let armors wayte preffe downe the
    burd'ned earth,
My foes, with wondring eyes fhall fee I over-prize my death.
But fince ye all (for all, I hope, alike affected bee, ..
Your wives, your children, lives, and land, from fervitude to
    free)
Are armed both in fhew and zeale, then glorioufly contend,
To winne and weare the home-brought fpoyles, of Victorie
    the end.
Let not the Skinners daughter Sonne poffeffe what he pre-
    tends,
He lives to die a noble death that life for freedome fpends."

I 4   Duke

Duke W I L L I A M's Speech.

" TO live upon or lie within this is my ground or grave
(My loving Souldiers), one of twaine your Duke refolves
to have.
Nor be ye *Normanes* now to feeke in what you fhould be ftout,
Ye come amidft the Englifh pikes to hewe your honors out,
Ye come to winne the fame by launce, that is your owne by
law,
Ye come, I fay, in righteous warre revenging fwords to draw.
Howbeit of more hardie foes no paffed flight hath fpead
yee,
Since Rollo to your now-abode with bands victorious lead
yee,
Or Turchus, Sonne of Troylus, in Scythian Fazo bread
yee.
Then worthy your progenitors yee Seede of Pryam's fonne
Exployt this Buifneffe, Rollons do that which yee wifh be
done.
Three people have as many times got and forgone this fhore,
It refteth now yee conquer it not to be conquered more:
For Normane and the Saxon blood conjoyning, as it may,
From that conforted feede the Crowne.fhall never paffe away,
Before us are our armed foes, behind us are the feas,
On either fide the foe hath holdes of fuccour and for eafe :
But that advantage fhall returne their difadvantage thus,
If ye obferve no fhore is left the which may fhelter us,
And fo hold out amidft the rough whil'ft they hale in for lee,
Whereas, whil'ft men fecurely fayle, not feldome fhipwracks
bee,

What

What fhould I cite your paffed acts, or tedioufly incence
To prefent armes; your faces fhew your hearts conceive
   offence,
Yea, even your courages devine a conqueft not to faile.
Hope then your Duke doth prophecie, and in that hope
   prevaile.
A people brave, a terren Heaven, both objects worth your
   warres,
Shall be the prizes of your prow's, and mount your fame
   to Starres.
Let not a Traytor's perjur'd Sonne extrude us from our
   right :
He dyes to live a famous life, that doth for conqueft fight."

Warner's Albion's Engl.
22 Chap. 4 B. 1602. Ed.

NORFOLK's Soliloquy before the Battle of

BOSWORTH.

" IF all the Campe prove traytours to my Lord,
   Shall fpotleffe Norfolke falfifie his word ?
Mine oath is paft, I fwore t' uphold his crowne,
And that fhall fwim, or I with it will drowne.
It is too late now to difpute the right,
Dare any tongue, fince Yorke fpread forth his light,
Northumberland, or Buckingham defame,
Two valiant Cliffords, Roos, or Beaumont's name,

5

Becaufe

Becaufe they in the weaker quarrell die ?
They had the King with them, and fo have I,
But ev'ry eye the face of Richard fhunnes,
For that foule murder of his brother's fonnes :
Yet lawes of Knighthood gave me not a fword
To ftrike at him, whom all with joint accord
Have made my Prince, to whom I tribute bring :
I hate his vices, but adore the King.
Victorious Edward, if thy foule can heare
Thy fervant Howard, I devoutly fweare,
That to have fav'd thy children from that day,
My hopes on earthe fhould willingly decay;
Would Gloucefter then, my perfect faith had tryed,
And made two graves, when noble Haftings died."

Bofworth Field, p. 7.

King R I C H A R D's Speech.

———— " M Y fellow Souldiers, though your fwords
Are fharpe, and need not whetting by my words ;
Yet call to minde thofe many glorious dayes,
In which we treafur'd up immortal prayfe.
If when I ferv'd, I ever fled from foe,
Fly ye from mine, let me be punifht fo :
But if my Father, when at firft he try'd
How all his fonnes could fhining blades abide,
Found me an Eagle, whofe undazled eyes
Affront the beames, which from the fteele arife,
And if I now in action teach the fame,
Know then, ye have but chang'd your Generall's name.

I   Be

Be ftill yourfelves, ye fight againft the droffe
Of thofe, that oft have runne from you with loffe.
How many Somerfets, diffentions brands,
Have felt the force of our revengefull hands !
From whome this Youth, as from a princely floud,
Derives his beft, yet not untainted blood.
Have our affaults made Lancafter to droupe ?
And fhall this Welfhman with his ragged troupe
Subdue the Norman and the Saxon line,
That onely Merlin may be thought divine ?
See what a guide thefe fugitives have chofe,
Who, bred among the French, our ancient foes,
Forgets the Englifh language, and the ground,
And knowes not what our drums and trumpets found !"

Sir J. Peaumont's Poems.
Lond. Ed. 1629.

Earl RICHMOND's Speech.

" IT is in vaine, brave friends, to fhew the right
Which we are forc'd to feeke by civill fight.
Your fwords are brandifht in a noble caufe,
To free your Country from a Tyrant's jawes.
What angry Planet, what difaftrous figne
Directs Plantagenet's afflicted line ?
Ah, was it not enough, that mutuall rage
In deadly battels fhould this race ingage,
Till by their blowes themfelves they fewer make,
And pillers fall, which France could never fhake ?

But

But muſt this crooked Monſter now be found,
'To lay rough hands on that uncloſed wound ?
His ſecret plots have much increaſt the flood,
He, with his brother's, and his nephewes blood,
Hath ſtain'd the brightneſſe of his Father's flowres,
And made his own white Roſe as red as ours.
This is the day, whoſe ſplendour puts to flight
Obſcuring clouds, and brings an age of light.
We ſee no hindrance of thoſe wiſhed times,
But this Uſurper, whoſe depreſſing crimes
Will drive him from the mountaine where he ſtands,
So that he needs muſt fall without our hands.
In this we happy are, that by our armes
Both Yorke and Lancaſter revenge their harmes.
Here Henry's ſervants joyne with Edward's friends,
And leave their privat griefes for publicke ends."

Sir J. Beaumont.

SPEECH of. VOADA, Queen of the
BRITTONS, before the Battle with the
ROMANS.

"MY ſtate and ſex, not hand or hart, moſt valiant Friends,
with-hild
Me (wretched cauſe of your repaire, by wicked Romans il'd)
From that revenge which I do wiſh, and ye have cauſe to
worke:
In which ſuppoſe not Voada in female feares to lurke.
For, loe, myſelfe, unlike myſelfe, and theſe ſame Ladies faire
In armor, not to ſhrinke an ynch wheare hotteſt doings are.
Even we do dare to bid the baſe, and you yourſelves ſhall ſee
Your ſelves to come behind in armes: the Romaines too
that be
Such Conquerors, and valiantlie can womankind oppreſſe,
Shall know that Brittiſh women can the Romiſh wrongs re-
dreſſe.
Then arme ye with like courages as Ladies ſhall preſent,
Whom ye, nor wounds, nor death, the praiſe of onſet ſhall
prevent.
Nor envie that our martiall rage exceeds your manly ire,
For by how much more we endure, ſo much more we deſire
Revenge, on thoſe in whoſe default we are unhallowed thus,
Whilſt they forget themſelves for men, or to be borne of us:
Ye

Ye yeeld them tribute, and from us their Legions have their
    pay;
Thus were too much, but more then thus, the haughtie
    Tirant's fway;
That I am Queene from being wrong'd doth nothing me
    protect:
Their rapes againft my Daughters both I alfo might object:
They maydes deflower, they wives enforce, and ufe their wils
    in all,
And yeat we live, defferring fight, inferring fo our fall.
But valiant Brutons, venttous Scots, and warlike Pichts, I
    erre,
Exhorting whom I fhould dehort, your fiearcenes to deferre:
Leffe courage more confiderate would make your foes' to
    quake:
My heart hath joy'd to fee your hands the Romaine ftandards
    take.
But when as force and fortune fail'd, that you with teeth
    fhould fight,
And in the faces of their Foes your women, in defpight,
Should fling their fuckling Babes, I hild fuch valiantnes but
    vaine:
Inforced flight is no difgrace, fuch flyers fight againe.
Here are ye, Scots, that with the King, my valiant Brother
    dead,
The Latines, wondring at your prowes, through Rome in
    triumph led:
Ye Mars-ftar'd Pichtes of Scythian breed are here colleagues,
    and more,
Ye Dardane Brutes, laft named, but in valour meant before:
In your conduct, moft knightly Friends, I fuperfeade the
    reft:
Ye come to fight, and we in fight to hope and helpe our beft."
                    Warner's Alb. Eng.
                    Chap. 18. B. 3. 1602.

MUTIUS

MUTIUS SCÆVOLA to PORSENNA.

" BEHOLD, grim Tyrant, here before thee ſtands
A man had been thy death, had not theſe hands
Prov'd traitours to my mind: had made that grave
Been thine, which now's prepared for thy ſlave.
If Scævola muſt undergo death's doom,
There's none but will write guiltleſſe on his tomb :
I ſet upon with fearleſſe courage thoſe
Who were our Capitols, our Countrie's foes.
Why are the Heavens then thus againſt me bent ;
And not propitious to my brave intent :
What, are the Gods aſham'd to lend their aid ;
Or are they of this Tyrant's pow'r afraid ?
Or have the Fates reſerved him that he
In future triumphs might a trophie be ?
Whate'er 'twas made them thus 'gainſt me conſpire,
It grieves my ſoul it had not its deſire.
Etruria, ſee what ſouls the Romans bear,
Admire the noble acts the Latians dare ;
Long after me that will this fact yet do,
There comes an other and an other too ;
There want not thoſe who hope to ſay they wore
A lawrel died in thy crimſon gore :

What

What though thy camp lies free from our alarms,
And fpoils our fields with unrevenged harms ;
We fcorn with bafer blood to ftain a dart,
O King, that's onely level'd at thy heart :
Our nobler fwords will drink the blood of none,
But thy heart-blood, Porfenna, thine alone ;
Thofe who their hands will ftrait in it imbrue,
Walk intermixed with thy armed crew.
Methinks I fee at prefent one thee note,
Who ftrait wil hide his weapon in thy throat ;
Hence, therefore, think each hower of thy breath,
To be th' affured hower of thy death ;
Thou doft with warlike troups our wals furround,
Hoping to lay them level with the ground,
And thinkft to famifh us, whilft o'er thy head,
Hangs a revengeful arm will ftrike thee dead ;
That glorious diadem which now I fee
Circles thy brow, was hop'd a fpoil by mee ;
That purple robe invefts thy loins fhal lie,
Thy blood be tinged in a deeper dy :
That very fcepter which thy hand fuftains,
Shal, turn'd a club, dafh out thy curfed brains ;
Now rule, now lord and king it, with this fate,
Expecting ftill the period of thy date.
Methinks I fee how on thy curled brow,
Self-rendring Vengeance fits enthron'd, and how
Thy thoughts already tear me ; yet I feel
No horror, nor my frighted body reel,
No trembling in my joynts ; know, king, I can
Both do and fuffer bove the reach of man :
In free born fouls pale terror never ftood
In competion with their Countries good ;
Thofe fouls in whom afpiring fame her fphear
Hath plac't, neglect the precipice of fear ;
This facred altar, thefe pure fires fhall be
Witneffes'of our undaunted conftancy ;

"This hand to Roman freedom fo unjuft,
Shall for its penance be confum'd to duft;
Nor is it cruel, but moft right its doom,
Since liberty it could not yield to Rome."

> John Dancer's Poems.
> Ed. 1660.

A Reconciliation effected between the two brothers, BRENN and BELINE, at the interceffion of
their Mother CONUVENNA.

"I Dare to name ye Sonnes, becaufe I am your Mother, yet
I doubt to tearme you Brothers that doe brotherhood
forget.
Thefe prodigies, their wrothfull fhields, forbodden foe to
foe,
Doe ill befeeme allyed hands, even yours allyed foe.
O, how feeme Oedipus his Sonnes in you againe to ftrive?
How feeme thefe fwords in me (aye me) Jocafta to revive?
I would Dunwallo lived, or ere death, had loft againe
His Monarchie, fufficing fower, but now too fmall for'twaine.
Then either would you, as did he, imploy your wounds elf-
wheare:
Or for the fmalnes of your power, agree at leaft for feare.

But pride of ritch and romefome Thrones, that wingeth now
    your darts,
It will (I would not as I feare) worke forrow to your harts.
My Sonnes, fweet Sonnes, attend my words, your Mother's
    wordes attend,
And for I am your Mother, doe conclude I am your frend :
I cannot counfell, but intreate, nor yet I can intreate
But as a woman, and the fame whofe blood was once your
    meate :
Hence had ye milke (fhe baerd her paps) thefe armes did
    hug ye oft :
Thefe fyled hands did wipe, did wrap, did rocke, and lay ye
    foft :
Thefe lips did kiffe, or eyes did weep, if that ye were un-
    queat,
Then ply I did, with fong, or fighes, with dance, with tung,
    or tente :
For thefe kind caufes, deere my Sonnes, difarme yourfelves :
    if not,
Then for thefe bitter teares that now your Mother's cheekes
    do fpot :
Oft urge I Sonnes and Mothers names, names not to be
    forgot.
Send hence thefe Souldiers : yec, my Sons, and none but yee
    fhould fight :
When none fhould rather be as one, if Nature had her
    right.
What comfort, Beline, fhall I fpeede ? fweete Brenn fhall I
    prevaile ?
Say yea, fweete Youthes, ah yea, fay yea : or if I needes muft
    faile,
Say noe : and then will I begin your battell with my baile,
Then then fome ftranger, not my Sonnes, fhall clofe me in the
    Earth
When we by armor over foone fhall meet, I feare, in death."

This

This fayd, with gufhing teares eftfoones fhe plyes the one
    and other,
Till both did fhew themfelves at length Sonnes worthy fuch a
    Mother :
And with thofe hands, thofe altred hands, that lately threatned
    bloes,
They did embrace: becomming thus continuall friends of
    foes.

                 Warner, Alb. Eng.
                 Chap. 16. B. 3.

N O T E S.

————

VOLUME I.

Page 2.   Wring her white hands, &c.

Thus Johnfon. Yet Vane could tell what ills from Beauty fpring;
And Sedley curs'd the form that pleas'd the King.
                                        Vanity of Hum. Wifh.

See likewife page 67, where Rofamond has the fame reflection.

Page 4.   Thefe lines of Fletcher are a paraphrafe, or rather tranflation from Boethius. The whole defcription is forcible: fome of the circum-ftances perhaps are heightened too much; but it is the fault of this writer to indulge himfelf in every aggravation that Poetry allows, and to ftretch his prerogative of " quidlibet audendi" to the utmoft. This fubject, verfi-fied in a very inferior ftyle, occurs in his Poetical Mifcellanies, p. 79, fub-joined to the P. Ifland.—For the effects of mufic on the Infernal Regions it may be almoft impertinent to refer the reader to the ftory of Orpheus, 4 Georg. Virgil; and the very mafterly introduction of it by Pope in his Ode on St. Cecilia s Day. The fame effect is reprefented by Horace as produced by the harps of Sappho and Alcæus, 2 Lib. 13 Od. 33. See alfo his Ode to Mercury, 3 Lib. 11 Od. 15. &c. See likewife Milton's P. Loft, 2 B. 546. 555.

Page 6.   This defcription was immediately taken from Spenfer's Bower of Blifs, F. Queen. 11 B. 12 Canto; upon ideal Paradifes of the kind, the beft Poets in almoft all ages and nations have lavifhed their defcriptive powers. Homer has his Gardens of Alcinous, and Virgil his Elyfium, Ariofto his Ifland of Alcina, and Taffo his Garden of Armida, Camoens his Garden of Venus, Marino his Gardens of Adonis, and laftly, Du Bartas and
Milton

Milton their Gardens of Eden. Thofe who wifh for minute and deferimi-native information on this fubject, are referred to Mickle's Differtation. See Lufiad, page 424.

Yet ftately *portance,* &c.

Thus Milton of Eve,

———————— She Delia's felf
In gait furpafs'd, and Goddefs-like *deport.*   B 9. P. L. 389.

There *port* was more than human, as they ftood.   Comus, 297.

Page 7.   The inner portch feem'd entrance to intice.
                    See Spenfer, St. LIII. LIV. 11 B. 12 Cant.

Page 8.   Which *ftellified* the roofe with painted colour.

A word in ufe amongft the Poets of that day. Drayton has it in his Legend of Matilda:

By him who ftrives to *ftellify* her name.

Again in Drummond:

With rofes here fhe *ftellifyed* the ground.   Son. 41.

Jetting Jacks. The word *jetting* feldom occurs applied to a perfon; it feems here to imply that reftlefs and unfettled ftate peculiar to idlenefs. It is ufed by Quarles, defcribing the Haggard: he fays, that fhe

Jets oft from perch to perch—   1 Emb. 3 B.

Sylvefter in his tranflation of Du. Bartas, has borrowed many of Niccol's lines from this defcription, which he has printed with very flight alterations, and amongft other expreffions he applies this to Vice. It will be fufficient to refer to the paffage, fee Fol. Edit. 1641. Lond. p. 101. *Jacks* is a com-mon expreffion denoting contempt with our older writers. Thus in the Mirror for Magiftrates we meet with

No golden churle, no elbow-vanting *Jacke.*   p. 565.

We ftill fay contemptuoufly, " a Jack in Office."

Page 9.   ——— ——— *flickering* eye.

A very expreffive epithet; it is ufed by Dyer in his truly claffical Poem, the Flecce, to denote the tremulous and fluctuating motion of the waves:

Till, rifing o'er the *flickering* wave, the Cape
Of Finefterre, &c.   4 B.

The concluding circumftances of this Piece are literally taken from Spen-fer, whofe exquifite lines will not it is hoped, be confidered as unneceffary here.

Eftfoons

Eftfoons they heard a moft melodious found
Of all that mote delight a dainty ear,
Such as at once might not on living ground,
Save in this Paradife, be heard elfewhere:
Right hard it was for wight which did it hear,
To read what manner mufick that mote be;
For all that pleafing is to living ear,
Was there conforted in one harmony,
Birds, voices, inftruments, winds, waters, all agree.

The joyous birds, fhrouded in chearful fhade,
Their notes unto the voice attemp'red fweet;
Th' angelical foft-trembling voices made
To th' inftruments divine refpondence meet :
The filver-founding inftruments did meet
With the bafe murmur of the waters fall :
The waters fall with difference difcreet,
Now foft, now loud, unto the wind did call :
The gentle-warbling wind low anfwered to all.   LXX. LXXI.

P. 10. In the edition of Chrift's Victory, together with the Purple Ifland, in 1783, many unwarrantable liberties are taken with the text, nor is
the leaft apology for the proceeding offered, or even the circumftance itfelf
mentioned. In almoft every page injuries are done to the fenfe, where im-
provements were intended. The republication feems to have originated
from a Letter of Harvey's (fee Let. Li. 2 vol.), and to have been executed
upon the ridiculous plan he there propofes. Now it is the indifpenfable
duty of every Editor of an ancient poet, to exhibit the fpelling of his author
in the exact ftate in which he found it, (unlefs indeed in fuch words as are
evidently miftakes of the prefs,) in order that the reader may trace the
progrefs of orthography, together with that of Poetry. Where this practice is not obferved, a republication is not merely imperfect but dangerous,
as it leads to an infinity of miftakes, and can anfwer no poffible end but that
of multiplying the number of our books without adding to the fources of our
information. Whoever therefore takes up the edition alluded to for the pur-
pofes of enjoying the poetry, making an extract, or a reference, can never
be fafe as to the authenticity of a fingle ftanza. A neat republication of all
Giles and Phineas Fletcher's Poetry from the old editions faithfully re-
printed, is much wanted.

Elonging joyfull day.

G. Fletcher has a fimilar term in the fame Poem. C 1. 41 Stan.

As when the cheerfull funne *elamping* wide.

It is in vain to fearch for either of thefe expreffions in the Modern Edition,
as they are there thus altered :

As when the cheerfull fun, *light fpreading wide.*
                                    37 St. C. 1. Mod. Ed.

K 4   *Keeping*

Keeping back joyful day.

Drummond in his profe works ufes *evanifhing*. See p. 222. Edin. Edit. 1711.
" Riches being momentary and *evanifhing*."
The moft material features of this defcription are taken from Spenfer.
F. Queen. B. 1. C. 9. Stan. 33, 36. This is a curious inftance of Plagiarifm,
and ferves to fhew us what little ceremony the Poets of that day laboured
under in pilfering from each other. The reader will be amply repaid for
his trouble in turning to the paffage in Spenfer, who feems to have put forth
all his ftrength to render the picture complete, and it is in delineations of
fuch a hue that he peculiarly excells. The limits of my book will not permit me to quote the paffage at length. See alfo Britannia's Paftorals by
Browne, vol. I. p. 162, Thomp. Edit.

Page 13.   And on their mafts where off the fhip-boy ftood,
— — — — — — — — — — — — —
            Some wearyed crow is fet.

This Image reminds us of a very fpirited paffage in Churchill :

            Let cormorants in churches make their neft,
            And on the fails of Commerce bitterns reft.   Go THAM.

            ——————— intreating at his doore
            For feme reliefe whom he fecured before——

a ftriking circumftance, perfectly fimilar to a well-known paffage of
Young :

            Some for hard mafters, broken under arms,
            In battle lopt away, with half their limbs,
            Beg bitter bread thro' realms their valour fav'd.   Night I.

Page 5.   Wifhing for death, and yet he could not die.

            Prayers are idle, Death is woo'd in vain ;
            In midft of death poore wretches long to die.
                              See Purple Ifland, C. 6. St. 37.

No Poet has exceeded Milton on this fubject, whofe lines are far too well
known to be here quoted :

            His cap borne up with ftaring of his haire.

            A very original incident.

    Mr. Hogarth, in his figure of Richard the Third, in the Tent Scene, has
reprefented the ring of the Tyrant as having ftarted beyond the joint of his
finger with the violent agitation of his frame. The incident is fuch as a
man of genius only could have conceived, though many look at the picture
without attending to the fublimity of it.

Page 17.   —— the ftill night's *feers* was he.

i. e. companion. Shakfpeare's eulogium on Sleep deferves a place here
as well for its beauty as its refemblance in fome degree to Sackville's :

                                                                    —— the

———————————— the innocent Sleep,
Sleep, that knits up the ravel'd fleave of Care,
The death of each day's life, fore labour's bath,
Balm of hurt minds, great Nature's fecond courfe,
Chief nourifher in Life's feaft.　　　　MACBETH.

Page 18.　The infirmities of Age are no where more emphatically enumerated than in Juvenal, 10 Sat. 190, &c.　Churchill, who has an exclufive right to the title of the Britifh Juvenal, has fome good lines on this fubject.　See his Gotham, B. 1. p. 11, 12. 3 vol.

Page 22.　And Priam eke in vaine, &c.
The death of Polites, 2 Æn. 526, 557. Virgil.　Which affords an excellent fubject for a picture ; but the Poet in his general account of the facking of Troy, preceding this particular defcription, has a circumftance relative to the death of Old Priam not fufficiently attended to as a beauty, yet eminently fine, and which is one of thofe few ftrokes that at once evince the fuperiority of Poetry over Painting :

　　Vidi Hecubam, centumque nurus Priamumque per aras
　　Sanguine fædantem, *quos ipfe facraverat ignes.*　　　501.

A fkilful Painter might have judicioufly felected a few of the moft interefting, and moft melancholy fpectacles of the night ; he might, by a proper difpofition of them, have fuccefsfully conveighed to our minds the diftrefs of Hecuba and her female attendants, at the fight of Pyrrhus and the two fons of Atreus ; all our finer feelings might have been fully excited by the dead Body of Priam himfelf, at the foot of the altar : but to have told us, that this very altar to which he had vainly fled for protection, and near which he now lay dead, had formerly, in the hour of peace and profperity, been confecrated by his own hand, would have baffled the powers of his pencil, and have forced from him a confeffion to this effect ; " Nobis non licet effe tam difertis !" Dr. Blair in his Lectures on Rhetoric, in his remarks on Virgil's talents for poetical defcription, expreffly felects this paffage, and obferves, that " The death of Priam, efpecially, may be fingled out as a mafter-piece of defcription." Vol. III. 169. but this the moft material circumftance feems to have efcaped him :

Page 25.　——————————— ordain'd to be
　　　　A lafting fame to Edward's victory.

His creft was three oftrich feathers ; and his motto, thefe German words, *Ich dien, I ferve,* which the Prince of Wales and his fuccelfors adopted in memorial of this great victory.　HUME.

Page 26.　Antonio Dorta.　SPEED.

Page 27.　In the time of May a variety of words were unfettled as to their accent, and were ufed either fhort or long, according to the will or neceffity of the Poet.　For inftance :

　　By this ftrict meanes were more *afcertain'd* there.
　　Muft *contribute* to Philip's overthrow.　　　　Page 26.

　　　　　　　　　　　　　　　　　　　　　Thus

Thus in Browne's Paſtorals:

Not that by mindes *commerce*, and joint eſtate.   B. I. Song 2.
In three Battalia's, &c. &c.

Holinſhed's account of the diſpoſition of the Engliſh Army, is as follows—" Then he ordeined three battels, in the firſt was the Prince of
Wales, and with him the Earl of Warwicke, the Lord Godfrey of Harecourt, the Lord S·afford, the Lord de la Ware, the Lord Bourchier, the
Lord Thomas Clifford, the Loı d Riginald Cobham, the Lord Thomas Hol-
land, Sir John Chandos, Sir Bartholomew Browaſh, Sir Robert Nevill.
They were eight hundred men of armes, and two thouſand archers, and a
thouſand of others, with the Welſhmen. In the ſecond battell was the Earle
of Northampton, the Earle of Arundell, the Lords Ros and Willowbie,
Baſſet, S. Albine, Multon, and others. The third battel the King led himſelfe, ha·ing with him ſeven hundred men of armes, and two thouſand
archers; and in the other battell even to the number of eight thouſand men
of armes, and twelve hunċred archers. Thus was the Engliſh armie mar-
ſhalled according to the report of Froiſſard." Chron. p. 371.

Page 28.   Darke grew the troubled ayre, &c. &c.

Both Speed and Holinſhed mention this. The following extraċt is from
the latter: " Alſo at the ſame inſtant there fell a great raine, and an
eclipſe with a terrible thunder, and before the raine there came flieng over
both armies a great number of crowes, for feare of the tempeſt coming."
P. 372.

Twixt both the Marſhalls, &c. &c.

Thus placed to the beſt advantage, King Edward viſiteth the ranckes in
perſon, riding upon a pleaſant hobby (having onely a white rod in his
hand, as if he would chaſtiſe fortune) betweene the two Marſhalls of his
field: whoſe very preſence, with a few ſeaſonable and unenforced words
on behalfe of God and his right, in ſteed of long orations, did inſpire the
fainteſt hearts among them with freſheſt vigour and alacritie. Speed, 577

Page 32.   *Horror* in all her ſaddeſt ſhapes appear'd.

Sir P. Sidney has a very ſublime deſcription of a field of Battle: " And
now the often changing fortune began alſo to change the hue of the battels;
for, at the firſt, though it were terrible, yet terror was decked ſo bravely
with rich furniture, gilt ſwords, ſhining, armours, pleaſant pencils, that
the eye with delight had ſcarce leiſure to be afraid: but now all univerſally
defiled with duſt, broken armour, mangled bodies, took away the maſk,
and ſet forth Horror in his own horrible manner.

Pemb. Arcadia, B. III. 446.

Page 33.   But moſt the warrelike Monarch of Boheme, &c. &c.

The circumſtance of his valiant death, and the flight of his ſon, is thus
mentioned by Holinſhed:—The valiant king of Bohem being almoſt blind,
cauſed his men to faſten all the reins of the bridels of their horſes ech to
other, and ſo he being himſelfe amongſt them in the foremoſt ranke, they
ran on their enemies. The lord Charles of Boheme, ſonne to the ſame
king,

king, and late elected emperour, came in good order to the battel ; but when he saw how the matter went awrie on their part, he departed and saved himself. His father, by the means aforesaid, went so far forward, that, joining with his enemies, he fought right valiantlie, and so did all his companie : but finallie being entred within the preafe of their enemies, they were of them inclofed and flaine, together with the king their mafter, and the next daie found dead, lieng about him, and their horfes all tied each to other. P. 372.

The attitude May has reprefented the brave old King as found in, is a very fine one :

> His cold dead hand did yet that fword retaine
> Which living erft it did fo bravelie wield.

One of the fineft of the Marlborough gems, a copy of which collection was fome fhort time fince prefented by the Duke to the Bodleian Library, is a dying Amazon ; fhe is drawn as juft falling from her horfe, and fupported by an attendant in all the languor of death, but ftill grafping her bow in her right hand. In the very elegant explanation that accompanies the plate are thefe words : " *Penthefileam effe creditur : quæ licet fpiritum ægrè trahens nondum tamen arcum e manu emifit.*" 48 Gem. Some of the moft remarkable and moft ftriking beauties in Poetry, Painting, and Statuary, are taken immediately from the agonies of Death. Virgil has a circumftance in this way full of horrid minutenefs, which is by fome confidered as a blemifh, but furely too faftidioufly :

> Te decifa fuum, Laride, dextera quærit
> Semianimefque micant digiti *ferrumque retraflant*. ÆN. X. 395.

The fame Poet, in defcribing the arms of Minerva, reprefents the Medufa on her breaft-plate as ftill rolling its eyes after the head is fevered from the neck :

> ——————————— ipfamque in pectore Divæ
> Gorgona, *defecto vertentem lumina collo*. Æn. VIII. 437.

For remarks on fimilar fubjects, fee Mr. Spence's moft excellent Effay on the Odyffey, p. 44, 45.

Page 34.   A moft compleat and glorious victory.

The flaughter of the Frenchmen was great and lamentable, namelie for the loffe of fo manie nobleman, as were flaine at the fame battell, fought between Creffie and Broy on the faturdaie next following the feaft of Saint Bartholomew being (as that yeare fell) the 26th. of Auguft. Among others which died that daie, thefe I find regiftered by name as cheefeft, John King of Boheme, Rafe Duke of Lorraine, Charles of Alanfo, brother germane to King Philip, Charles Earle of Blois, Lewis Earl of Flanders, alfo the Earle of Harecourt, brother to the Lord Geoffrie of Harcourt ; with the Earles of Auffere, Aumerle, and Saint Poule, befides diverfe other of the nobilitie. Holinfhed's Chron, 372. The number of the flain (according to Hume) was as follows ; " Cn the day of battle, and on the enfuing, there fell, by a moderate computation, 1200 French

Knights,

Knights, 1400 gentlemen, 4000 men at arms, befides about 30,000 of inferior rank."—On the fide of the Englifh, he fays, " there were killed in it only one Efquire, and three Knights, and a very few of inferior rank."

Pages 35 and 36. Thefe beautiful lines feem to have fuggefted the plan of a moft exquifite little piece called " *The Hamlet*," by Mr. T. Warton, which contains fuch a feleçtion of beautiful rural images as perhaps no other poem of equal length in our language prefents us with. The latter part of it more clofely reminds us of Fletcher. A fhepherd's life is to be found in Spenfer's Fairy Queen, B. VI. Cant. 9, St. 20. See likewife J. Sylvefter's Tranflation of Du Bartas. Ed. 1641. page 29, 30.

Page 37. It may not be amifs to fet before the reader a few extraçts from our old Hiftorians, relative to the caftle of Nottingham, and the capture of Mortimer there. " There was in the caftle of Nottingham (and at this day is), a certaine fecret way or mine cut through a rocke, upon which the faid caftle is built, one iffue whereof openeth toward the river Trent, which runnes under it, and the other venteth itfelfe farre within upon the furface, and is (at this prefent) called *Mortimer's* hole ; through this the young King, well armed and ftrongly feconded, was conduçted with drawne fwords, by fome his trufty and fworne fervants (among which was that brave Montacute, whom his virtues under this King raifed to the Earledome of Salifbury, &c. &c.) up to the Queene's chamber, whofe dore (fo fearlefs is blinded affeçtion) was unfhut, and with her was Mortimer ready to goe to bed, whom, with the flaughter of a Knight, and one er two that refifted, they laid hold upon. This was not reputed a a flender enterprife, in regard, that in Mortimer's retinue were not fewer (they fay) then one hundredth and fourfcore Knights, befides Efquires and Gentlemen. Speed's Chron. Ed. 1627, p. 580."

Leland, in his Itinerary, gives a very particular account of the place, but too long for infertion here. What direçtly relates to Mortimer is this " The dungeon or kepe of the Caftel ftondith by South and Eft, and is exceeding ftrong *et natura loci et opere*. Ther is an old fair chapelle, and a welle of a gret depthe; and there is alfo a chochlea with a turret over it, wher the kepers of the Caftella fay Edwarde the thirdes band cam up thorough the rok, and toke the Earle Mortymer Prifoner. Ther is yet a faire ftaire to go downe by the rok to the ripe of line." Hearne's Edit, fol. 3, 1745. Holinfhed's account is the following ;—In a parlement holden at Notingham, about faint Luke's tide, Sir Roger Mortimer, the earle of March, was apprehended the feventeenth day of Oçtober, within the caftell of Notingham, where the king with the two queenes, his moţther and his wife, and diverfe other were as then lodged, and though the keies of the caftell of Notingham were dailie and nightlie in the cuftodie of the faid earle of March, and that his power was fuch, as it was doubted how he might be arrefted (for he had, as fome writers affirme, at that prefent in retinue nine fcore knights, befides efquires, gentlemen and yeomen) yet at length by the king's helpe, the lord William Montacute, the lord Hvmfrie de Bohun, and his brother Sir William, the lord Rafe Stafford, the lord Robert Clifford, the lord William Clinton, the lord John Nevill of Hornbie, and diverfe other, which had accufed the faid earle of March for tne murther of king Edward the fecond, found means by intelligence had with Sir William de Cland, conftable of the caftell of

Notingham, to take the said earle of March, with his sonne the lord Roger or Geffrey Mortimer, and Simon Hereford, with other. — Sir Hugh Trumpington (or Turrington as some copies have), that was one of his cheefest freends, with certaine other, were slaine as they were about to resist against the lord Montacute and his company in taking of the said earle. The manner of his taking I passe over, bicause of the diversitie in report thereof by sundrie writers. From Notingham he was sent up to London with his sonne the lord Roger or Geoffry de Mortimer, Sir Simon Bereford, and the other prisoners, where they were committed to prison in the Tower. Shortlie after was a parlement called at Westminster, theefelie (as was thought) for reformation of things disordered through the misgovernance of the earle of March. But whosoever was glad or sorie for the trouble of the said earle, suerlie the queene mother took it most heavilie above all other, as she that loved him more (as the fame went) than stood with her honour. For as some write, she was found to be with child by him. They kept, as it were, house togither ; for the earle, to have his provision the better cheape, laid his pen·e with hirs, so that hir takers served him as well as they did hir, both of vittels and carriages ; of which misusage (all regard to honour and estimation neglected) everie subject spake shame. For their manner of dealing, tending to such evill purposes as they continuallie thought upon, could not be secret from the eies of the people, and their offense heerein was so much the more heinous, because they were persons of an extraordinarie degree and were the more narrowlie marked of the multitude or common people. P. 349.

Page 39. ———— an *estate* of lawn.

That is, a *canopy* of lawn. *State* was the word more commonly used.

> His high throne which under *state*
> Of richest texture. Book X, p. 441, Paradise Lost.

Page 46. And through the *ragged entrails* of the cave.

Thus Shakespeare in a much-admired simile :

> Which like a taper in some monument
> Doth shine upon the dead man's earthy checks,
> That shews the *ragged entrails* of this pit.
>
> Titus And. Scene VI.

Page 47. Carnarvon Edward's manes had possest
The roome, &c. &c.

On Mortimer's impeachment, the first of the five articles laid to his charge, was, " That he had procured Edward of Carnarvon, the king's father, to be murthered, in most heinous and tyrannous manner, within the castel of Berklie." Holinshed, p. 349.

Page 48. Dear Son (for well she knew her son was there), &c. &c.

May seems here to have consulted Stow in his account. " Upon a certaine night, the king lying without the castle (Nottingham) both he and his friends were brought by torch light through a secret way under ground, be-

beginning far off from the fayde caftle, till they came even to the Queenes chamber, which they by chance found open : they therefore being armed with naked fwords in their hands, went forwards leaving the king alfo armed without the doore of the chamber, leaft that his mother fhoulde efpie him : they which entred in flew *Hugb Turpington*, knight, who refifted them, Mafter *John Newel* of Horn, by giving him his deadly wound. From thence they went toward the Queene Mother, whom they found with the earle of March readie to have gone to bedde : and having taken the fayde Earle, they ledde him ont into the hall, after whom the Queene followed, crying, *Bel filz, Bel filz, ayes pitie de gentil Mortimer :* Good fonne, good fonne, take pittie upon gentle Mortimer, for fhe fufpeded that her fonne was there, though fhe faw him not." Chron. fol. 1615, p. 229.

Page 49. The particular relation that the whole of this Piece bears to many paffages in Milton's Paradife Loft, and the great fublimity of the Poetry, are reafons fufficient to make it acceptable to every reader of tafte, notwithftanding its being a tranflation. Of the *Sofpetto D'Herode* it is to be lamented, that poetical readers in general know fo little, from the fpecimen here produced, every Englifh reader muft be inclined to wifh for more. A very intelligent correfpondent in Maty's Review for March, 1785, (Article ; Phillip's Edition of Crafhaw) has told us, that the whole Poem has already been rendered into Englifh verfe, and that the title-page of the tranflation ftands thus. " The flaughter of the Innocents by Herod ; written in Italian by the famous poet the Cavalier Marino, in four books, newly Englifhed, 1675 ; to which is added in my copy in writing, " Englifhed by T. R ;" to whom the initials T. R. belong I know not ; but the tranflation feems fuperior to Crafhaw."——An Epitome of the 2d book is then given. Surely a republication of this Tranflation would be highly worth republifhing, particularly if executed in a fuperior ftyle to Crafhaw, which feems to me hardly poffible :

His eyes the fullen dens of Death and Night, &c.

Milton gives him

———— eyes
That fparkling blaz'd.   193. 1 B.

Milton has this fimile of a Comet in his 2d Book.

———— on th' other fide,
Incens'd with indignation Satan ftood,
Unterrify'd; *and like a comet,* burn'd,
That fires th' Arctic fky, and from his horrid hair
Shakes peftilence and war.   — 710

Again, he compares him to the fun in an Eclipfe. 598. 1 B. P. Loft.

Page 50. While his fteel fides found with his tail's ftrong lafh.

Thus Milton fpeaking of the Old Dragon, upon the very fame occafion :

Swindges the fcaly horrour of his tail.
                                        Hymn of the Nativ. 18 Stan
                                                                              Pag

Page 51. He faw rich nectar thaws releafe the rigor, &c.

For an oppofite, picture to this, fee Shakfpeare's Midfum. Night's Dream.

———— —— hoary-headed frofts
Fall in the frefh lap of the crimfon rofe ;
And on old Hyem's chill and icy crown
An od'rous chaplet of fweet fummer buds
Is as in mockery fet.   Act. 2. Sc. 2.

Page 52. He faw the falling idols all confefs
A coming Deity.

See Milton's Hymn on the Nativity, where thefe particulars are moft fublimely enumerated, IX Stan. &c. among other portents, that of the Oracles having been all ftruck dumb is not the moft inconfiderable. G. Fletcher, in his Chrift's Victorie, publifhed in 1610, fome time before Milton could poffiby have compofed his Ode, has a fimilar idea on the fame occafion :

The Angells caroll'd, low'd their fongs of peace,
The curfed Oracles war ftrucken dumb,
To fee their Shepheard, the poore fhepheards prefs,
To fee their King, the kingly Sophies come.   82 St. Can. 1.

For the fulleft information on this fubject, fee Mr. T. Warton's Edit. of Milton's Minor Poems, p. 280, to which this paffage may be added :

He fhook himfelf, and fpread *his fpacious wings*, &c.
In the fame ftyle Milton talks of *his fail-broad vans*. B 2. P. Loft.

Page 55. What though I mift my blow, &c.

Thus Milton :

———— — what though the field be loft ?
All is not loft ; th' unconquerable will,
And ftudy of revenge immortal hate,
And courage never to fubmit or yield. B. 1.

Phineas Fletcher thus, in a fimilar fpirit, defcribes the Dragon :

Yet full of malice and of ftubborn pride,
Though oft had ftrove, and had been foil'd as oft,
Boldly his death and certain fate defi'd :
And mounted on his flaggie fails aloft,
With boundleffe fpite he long'd to try again
A fecond loffe, and new death ; glad and fain
To fhew his pois'nous hate, though ever fhew'd in vain.

So up he rofe upon *his ftretched fails,*
Fearleffe expecting his approaching death :
So up he rofe, that th' ayer ftarts, and fails,
And over-preffed * finks his load beneath:
　　So up he rofe, as does a thunder-cloud,
　　Which all the earth with fhadows black does fhroud:
So up he rofe and through the weary ayer row'd.
　　　　　　　　　　　　　P. Ifland. 12 Can. 58. St.

See alfo a very fpirited Speech in G. Fletcher's Chrifts Triumph, Part 1.
20 Stan.

　　Page 58.　The image of Death, who is here defcribed as mafter of this
murderous groupe, being almoft out of breath with endlefs buifnefs, can
never be fufficiently commended :

　　　　The cup they drink in is Medufa's fcull.

This circumftance reminds us of a paffage in a Runic Ode preferved by
Olaus Wormius, the old Scandinavian warrior Lodbrog, difdaining life
and thinking on the joys of immortality, which he was foon about to fhare
in the hall of Odin, exclaims in a high fpirit of favage fublimity :

　　　　Bibemus cerevifiam
　　　　Ex concavis cranium crateribus.

　　Page 58.　They prick a bleeding heart at every ftitch.
This line muft immediately recall to the minds of the lovers of Gray, his
" Fatal Sifters," an Ode tranflated from the Norfe.

　　Page 59.　———————— a black wood
　　　　Which *nods* with many a heavy-headed tree.

　　　　And low-brow'd rocks hang *nodding* o'er the deeps.
　　　　　　　　　　　　　　　　　Pope's Eloifa.

　　Page 60.　————— tam'd the rebellious eye
　　　　Of forrow.

An expreffion of infinite beauty and force, it is ufed by fome one of our later poets; but I am now unable to turn to the paffage.

　　Page 61.　She thinks not fit fuch he her face fhould fee,

　　　　As it is feen by Hell, and feen with dread.

The reverfe of this, that is in a good fenfe, is Virgil's:

　　　　————— qualifque videri
　　　　Cælicolis et quanta folet.　　　　　　　　2 Æn.

* See Milton, 225, B. 1.　The original is to be found in Spenfer's
F. Queen, B. 1. Cant. 11. 18 Stan. where the air is reprefented as too light
to fupport the weight of the Old Dragon.　Sound was never more
completely rendered an echo to fenfe than in the laft line of the 2d
Stanza, which I have quoted from P. Fletcher :

　　" *So up he rofe and through the weary ayer rowd.*"

　　　　　　　　　　　　　　　　　　　　　　Page

Page 66. But fits at home *with folded arms.*

Shakfpeare, who above all others has the power of giving to common circumftances an air the moft uncommon, has a pretty image of this kind.
Ariel is defcribing to Profpero in what manner he had executed his orders :
amongft other things he adds :

> The King's fon have I landed by himfelf,
> Whom I left cooling of the air with fighs
> In an odd angle of the Ifle, and fitting
> *His arms in this fad knot.*   TEMPEST.

Page 67. ——————wifhing in vaine
> She could recall her virgine ftate againe.

Thus Rowe in his Jane Shore :
> In vain with tears her lofs fhe may deplore ;
> In vain look back to what fhe was before.

When that *unblemifh'd forme,*

Thus Milton in his Comus :

> And thou *unblemifh'd form* of Chaftity.   215.

He had originally written, " And thou *unfpotted forme* of Chaftity."
How far this expreffion of May might influence him in the alteration, it is
impoffible to determine :

> O ! then fhe wifh'd her beauties ne'er had been
> Renown'd ;——

I cannot refift the opportunity of quoting a few fine lines from Daniel on
this occafion, and on this very fubject :

> Did nature (for this good) ingeniate,
> To fhew in thee the glory of her beft ;
> *Framing thine eye the ftar of thy ill fate,*
> Making thy face the foe to fpoil the reft ?
> O Beauty, thou an enemy profeft
>   To chaftity, and us, that love thee moft,
>   Without thee, how w' are loath'd, and with thee loft ?
>   COMPL. OF ROSAMOND.

The *rofie tincture* her fweete cheekes forfooke.

Thus Milton,

> What need a *vermeil-tinctur'd* lip for that.   COMUS

The tale of Fair Rofamond is altogether moft happily adapted to the pur-
pofes of poetry, nor has it efcaped the notice of our older poets, for (exclufive of May) Warner, Drayton, and Daniel, have each tried their refpec-
tive powers upon it. P. Fletcher, in his P. Ifland, alludes to one of them,
though it is uncertain which, Cant. 5. Stan. XLV. Both Drayton and

Daniel mention the circumstance of King Henry's having presented Rosamond, the night before her ruin, with a casket wrought with the story of
Neptune and Amymone; this little incident is most probably from history.
The necessary curious information for illustrating the whole story may be
found in Dr. Percy's Reliques, vol. II. p. 141. who has entirely anticipated
me on the subject. It may be necessary to apprise some readers, that the
word Bower was formerly used with considerably greater latitude than at
present; and when applied to the residence of Rosamond, as it frequently
is, means simply, retreat, private abode, it annexs with it an idea of retirement, but no farther. Thus Spenser in his LXX Sonnet, invokes the
Spring :

> Go to my love, where she is careless laid,
> Yet in her Winter's *Bowre* not well awake.

The term occurs in almost every page of our old Poets, with the same
general signification. The word *Cabin* is used in a similar manner :

Page 71.   Look how a mother, &c.
> See Browne's Brit. Past. Song 4. B 2. first lines.

Page 73.   When others sleepe whych may enjoy their *makes*.

A common expression for *mates*. Thus Spenser, in his fine Sonnet to the
Spring :

> Where every one that misseth then her *make*.   LXX.

Page 74. My chosen *pheare*. Sometimes spelt *fere*, and is used indifferently for husband, lover, or companion :

> *My gem*, and all my joy.

An expression of endearment of great beauty. Thus Antony says in Shakspeare :

> Have I my pillow left unprest in Rome,
> Forborn the getting of a lawful race,
> And by a *gem* of women.   Sc. 11.

Page 77. She casting downe her bashfull eyes, &c.

These two lines contain the very soul of simplicity : they are in the writer's
best manner, and may safely vie with any modern lines on a similar
subject.

Page 78. Live safe, therefore, for in thy life consists the life of twaine.

Similarity of situation must unavoidably produce similarity of sentiment;
and consequently of expression : perhaps few readers will peruse this line
without immediately calling to mind the conclusion of a song considerably
too popular to be here introduced.

Page 79. Warner has here taken an opportunity of ridiculing the taſte
r Tilts and Tournaments, then ſo much in faſhion :

——————————*Tantara* to the fight.

hus Sylveſter, in his Tranſlation of Du Bartas :

A heav'nly trump, a ſhrill *Tantara* blowes.   173.

Page 80.   Dawlian bird :

Sola virum non ulta piè mœſtiſſima mater
Concinit Iſmarium *Daulius ales* Ityn.
Ales Ityn, Sappho deſertos cantat amores
Haſtenus, ut mediâ cætera noſte ſilent.

OVID. Saph. Ph. 153.

Page 84.   I finde my fault, but follow it, &c.

Thus Pope :

I view my crime, but kindle at the view.   ELOISA.

Page 90.   Wrong not thy fair youth, &c.
             See this argument purſued at large in Milton's Comus, 737, &c.

Page 91.   —————— my delicious cheek
             Tinſted with crimſon.

Expreſs'd with a delicate felicity, ſuperior to Milton's, " vermeil-tinſtur'd
ip," which it might have contributed perhaps originally to ſuggeſt ; but
Milton's very epithet occurs in the poetry of Ed. Benlowes.   1 Cant. St. 21.
1652. Fol. Edit.

Crouch low ! O *vermeil-tinſtur'd* cheek.

Page 93.   Forgotten as our fav ours in a glaſs.

A thought peculiarly in the ſtyle of Shakſpeare, yet, to the beſt of my
knowledge, unborrowed from him.   What follows, namely his comparing
the pleaſures of life to

A very tale of that which never was.

Is an improvement, I think, upon Shakſpeare's compariſon of life to

————————— a tale
Told by an ideot, full of found and fury,
Signifying nothing.   MACBETH, Scene 5.

Speed gives the following relation of this ſtory.   " King John diſherited
ſome noblemen without judgement of their peeres, and he would have deſtroyed Ranulph Earle of Cheſter, for that he reproched him with this,
that he ſhould uſe the wife of his brother Geffrey, Earle of B-ytaine,
whom Ranulph Earle of Cheſter had married, and from whom Ranulph

L 2   was

was divorced by the council of King John, and the said Earle had marrie the daughter of the Earle Ferrers. King John being now in extremit and mindinge to impute the fault to them that would not appeafe his fu: aforetime, reprehended fometimes one, and fometimes an other of his n bility, as traytors, calling them jealous, whofe beds (as he bragged) he h: defiled, and defloured their daughters. The Chronicle of Dunmow fait this difcord arofe betwixt the king and his barons becaufe of Mawde, call the faire, daughter to Robert Fitz Walter, whom the king loved, but h father would not confent, and thereupon enfued war throughout Englar. The king fpoiled efpecially the caftle Baynard in London, and other hol and houfes of the Barons. Robert Fitz Walter, Roger Fitz Robert, a Richard Mount Fitchet, paffed over into France; fome alfo went in Wales, and fome into Scotland, and did great damage to the king. While Mawde the Faire remained at Dunmow, there came a meffenger unto h from king John about his fuit in love; but becaufe fhe would not agree, t meffenger poifoned a boiled or potched egge againft fhe was hunger whereof fhe died, and was buried in the quire at Dunmow." Stow's A nales, 1615. Ed. p. 170.

Page 95.   As there we ftood, the countrie round we ey'd, &c.

If we confider the time in which this was written, we cannot but adm the juftnefs and propriety of the rural fcenery here felected.
How the *gray* fhepherd. The epithet *gray* refers to his drefs and not age. Thus Drayton defcribes the fame character:

The Shepheard ware a *fheepe-gray* cloke,
Which was of the fineft loke
That could be cut with fheere.   Dowsabell.

Page 100. This public entry of Henry and Bolinbroke, is thus int duced and defcribed by Shakfpeare.
Scene 3. *The Duke of York's Palace. Enter York and his Dutchef.*

Dutch. My Lord, you told me you would tell the reft,
When weeping made you break the ftory off,
Of our two coufins coming into London.
York. Where did I leave?
Dutch. At that fad ftop, my Lord,
Where rude mif-govern'd hands, from window tops,
Threw duft and rubbifh on King Richard's head.
York. Then, as I faid, the Duke, great Bolingbroke,
Mounted upon a hot and firey fteed,
Which his afpiring rider feem'd to know,
With flow but ftately pace kept on his courfe:
While all tongues cry'd, *God fave thee Bolingbroke!*
You would have thought the very windows fpake;
So many greedy looks of young and old
Through cafements darted their defiring eyes
Upon his vifage; and that all the walls

With painted imag'ry had said at once,
Jesu preserve thee! welcome, Bolingbroke!
Whilst he, from one side to the other turning,
Bareheaded, lower than his proud steed's neck
Bespoke them thus, " *I thank you, country-men;*"
And thus still doing, thus he pass'd along.
   Dutch. Alas! poor Richard, where rides he the while?
   York. As in a theatre, the eyes of men,
After a well-grac'd actor leaves the stage,
Are idly bent on him that enters next,
Thinking his prattle to be tedious:
Even so, or with much more contempt, men's eyes
Did scowl on Richard; no man cry'd, *God save him!*
No joyful tongue gave him his welcome home;
But dust was thrown upon his sacred head;
Which with such gentle sorrow he shook off,
His face still combating with tears and smiles,
The badges of his grief and patience;
That had not God, for some strong purpose, steel'd
The hearts of men, they must perforce have melted,
And barbarism itself have pitied him.
But Heaven hath a hand in these events,
To whose high will we bound our calm contents.
To Bolingbroke are we sworn subjects now,
Whose state and honour I for aye allow.   RICHARD II.

Page 102.   Are these the triumphs for thy victories?

ı the same spirit with Virgil's,

    Hi nostri reditus expectatique triumphi!   11 Æn. 54.

Page 106.   These heares, of age are messengers, &c.

e Dr. Percy's Ballads, who has printed the following fine traditional lines,
ing part of an old song which he professes to have received from a friend:

   ——— his reverend lockes
In comelye curles did wave;
And on his aged temples grewe
The blossomes of the grave.   p. 160. vol. II.

Page 107.   Were not the smother'd children buried deep?

here is much nature in this spirited interrogation.

Page 109.   ——— he takes his helmet bright,
    Which like a twinkling starre with trembling light
    Sends radiant lustre through the darksome aire:

his description of a piece of armour is as fine as any thing I am able to
collect of the kind. Let the reader compare it with the following lines
Glover:

——— his

———————————— his glittering fhield
Whofe fpacious orb collects th' effulgent beams
Which from his throne meridian Phœbus caft,
Flames like another fun.   LEONIDAS.

Page 113.   Thrice happy you, that look as from the fhore, &c.

Suave mari magno turbantibus æquora ventis,
E terrâ magnum alterius fpectare laborem;
Non quia vexari quemquam eft jucunda voluptas,
Sed quibus ipfe malis careas, quia cernere fuave eft.
                                        Lucret. 2 Lib

On the fubject of kindred fenfations to this, I have been always pleafed
with the following paffage in Dr. Johnfon's Journey to the Weftern Iflands
" We came in the afternoon to *Slanes Caftle*, built upon the margin of the
fea, fo that the walls of one of the towers feem only a continuation of a
perpendicular rock, the foot of which is beaten by the waves.   To walk
round the houfe feemed impracticable ; from the windows the eye wander
over the fea that feparates Scotland from Norway, and when the wind
beat with violence muft enjoy all the terrifick grandeur of the tempeftuous
ocean.   I would not for my amufement wifh for a ftorm ; but as ftorm,
whether wifhed or not, will fometimes happen, I may fay, without viola-
tion of humanity, that I fhould willingly look out upon them from Slanes
Caftle." p. 36.

N O T E S.

VOLUME II.

Page 3.   Keenly they hunted, &c.

To this and the fucceeding lines, may with juſtice be applied, what Dr. Warton has obſerved of ſome lines of Pope. " The metaphors in the ſucceeding lines, drawn from the field-ſports of ſetting and ſhooting, ſeem below the dignity of the ſubject." 2 Vol. 124, on Pope.

Page 6.   There is a moral charm in theſe little pieces of Southwell, that will prejudice moſt readers of feeling in favour of their author; ſhould theſe volumes meet with ſucceſs, the publiſher of them will make it his buiſneſs to collect and republiſh the better part of Southwell's poetry, which is now entirely forgotten, and very ſcarce. Bolton, in his Hypercritica, makes mention of him. " Never muſt be forgotten St. Peter'sComplaint, and thoſe other ſerious poems ſaid to be father Southwell's: the Engliſh whereof, as it is moſt proper, ſo the ſharpneſs and light of wit is very rare in them."

Page 9.   Whereon when as the gazing paſſenger, &c.

Pope had a ſimilar idea in his intended Ode on the Folly of Ambition, the ſketch of which is preſerv'd in Ruffhead, p. 424.

Page 9.   And there Ambri plac'd in memory, &c.

See Selden's Notes to Drayton's Poly Olbion. Song 3. Mr. Warton's Hiſt. of Eng. Poetry, 1 Vol. p. 53.

Page 10.   And are become a traitor to their name.

Thus Drayton speaking of the same place. Poly-Olbion, 3 Song.

> Ill did those mighty men to trust thee with their story
> That haft forgot their names, who rear'd thee for their glory :
> For all their wondrous coft, thou that haft ferv'd them fo,
> What 'tis to truft to tombs, by thee we eafily know.

Page 13.   ———— the *facred* luft of gold
     .   Now fires thy fpirit.

Sacred is here ufed in the fenfe of *accurfed* like the *auri facra fames* of Virgil. 3 Æn. 57.

Page 15.   But fince our life fo faft away doth flide, &c.

> Life's ftream for obfervation will not ftay,
> It hurries all too faft to mark their way :
> In vain fedate reflections we would make,
> When half our knowledge we muft fnatch, not take.
> On human actions reafon tho' you can,
> It may be reafon, but it is not man;
> His principles of action once explore,
> That inftant 'tis his principle no more.
>
> Pope's Epift. to Sir R. Temple.

Page 16.   Where is th' Affyrian Lion's golden hide, &c.

Thus Spenfer in " The Ruines of Time."

> What now is of th' Affyrian Lionefs,
> Of whom no footing now on earth appears ?
> What of the Perfian bear's outrageoufnefs,
> Whofe memory is quite worn out with years ?
> Who of the Grecian Libbard now ought hears,
>   That over-ran the Eaft with greedy powre,
>   And left his welps their Kingdoms to devour ?
>
> p. 9. Hugh. Edit.

> *And that black Vulture, which with deathfull wing*
> *Ore-fhadowes half the earth*————

Mr. Hayley, in his Effay on Hiftory, has a very bold and magnificent image of this kind. He is about to defcribe Livy, Ep. i.

> Of mightier fpirit, of majeftic frame;
> With powers proportion'd to the Roman fame,
> *When Rome's fierce Eagle his broad wings unfurl'd*
> *And fhadow'd with his plumes the fubject world*
> In bright pre-eminence, &c.

Page

Page 18.　Brave minds, oppreſt, ſhould in deſpight of fate,
　　　Lo.ke greateſt, like the ſune, in loweſt ſtate.

Blair has the ſame thought in his fine poem, the Grave, ſpeaking of the
death of the juſt man :

　　　By unperceiv'd degrees he wears away,
　　　Yet, like the ſun, ſeems larger at his ſetting.
　　　　　　　　　　　　　　　　　Edinb. Edit. p. 31.

Page 19.　——————*unflattered* age.

A very original epithet.

Page 20.　Yet know, what buſie path ſoere you tread
　　　To Gratneſſe, you muſt ſleepe among the dead.

How comprehenſively, how plainly, yet how ſublimely, hath Gray expreſſed
this trite ſentiment :

　　　The paths of glory lead but to the grave.　Church-yard.

Page 22.　With others I *commune*.　See note on p. 27. Vol. I.

Page 25.　——————could I vie
　　　Angels with India.

An *angel* is a piece of coin, value ten ſhillings.　The words *to vie angels*, are
a periphraſis, and ſignify *to compare wealth*.　See Sir J. Hawkins's note on
the paſſage, p. 264.　Walton's Comp. Angler—Cartwright uſes the word
Angel :

　　　You ſhall ne'r know what *angels*, peeces, pounds
　　　Theſe names of want and beggary mean ;—
　　　　　　　　　　　　　　　The Ordinary, Act 2. Sc. 3.

Page 27.　Read on this dial, &c.　No poet whatever has introduced this
circumſtance with the happineſs of Shakſpeare ; who compares the ſilent
and almoſt imperceptible flight of beauty, to the ſtealing ſhadow of a ſun-
dial.　As the lines are in one of his minor poems, they may probably have
eſcaped the notice of common readers :

　　　Ah yet doth Beautie like a dyall hand,
　　　Steale from his figure, and no place perceived ;
　　　So your ſweete hew, which me-thinks ſtill doth ſtand
　　　Hath motion, and mine eye may be deceived.
　　　　　　　　Conſtant Affection. Shak. Poems, 1640. Edit.

The verſes are incorrect, but the idea is fine—the ſhadow ſteals from the
dial's hand, and not the dial's hand from the ſhadow—

　　　My ſhort-lived winter's day !—

　　　　　　　　　　　　　　　　　　　　Dyer.

Dyer, in his well-known Grongar Hill, well denominates the fmile of Fate:

> A fun-beam in a winter's day.

For farther obfervations on this piece, fee Jackfon's very elegant and fenfible Letters. 2 Vol. 19 Let.

Page 28. *Flame-ey'd* Fury. An epithet highly original and fine. Shakfpeare ufes *fire-ey'd* Fury, in his Romeo and Juliet.

Page 29. For farther obfervations, fee 2 Vol. 30 Let. Jackfon's Letters, where both thefe particular pieces of Quarles were firft more immediately brought forward to the public eye.

Page 30. Thefe lines figned F. K. are probably written by Francis Kinwelmerfhe, a contributor to the collection in which they appear, and a ftudent of Grays-Inn. He affifted Gafcoigne in his Tragedy of Jocafta.

Page 34.　　But how may I this honour now attaine,
　　　　　　That cannot, &c.

> Well may they rife, while I, whofe ruftick tongue
> Ne'er knew to puzzle right, or varnifh wrong,
> Spurn'd as a beggar, dreaded as a fpy,
> Live unregarded, unlamented die.　　Johnfon's London.

Page 35.　　Grinne when he laughs, &c.
> To fhake with laughter ere the jeft you hear,
> To pour at will the counterfeited tear,
> And as their Patron hints the cold or heat,
> To fhake in dog-days, in December fweat.　　Johnfon's London.

Page 36.　　———————— and him true and playne,
　　　　　　That rayleth reachlefs unto eche man's fhame.

Thus Horace:

> ———————— at eft truculentior, atque
> Plus æquo liber; fimplex fortifque habeatur.　　3 Sat. 1 Lib. 51.

Page 40.　　And her eternall fame be read,
　　　　　　When all, but very Vertue's dead.

Somewhat in the manner of Collins:

> Belov'd, till life can charm no more;
> *And mourn'd till Pity's felf be dead.*　　DIRGE.

Page 41. I have always confidered this Epitaph as Carew's Mafterpiece. The fubject of it may poffibly be the fame perfon, to whofe nuptials with Lord Charles Herbert, Davenant has infcribed fome verfes. p. 238. Fol. Edit.

Page 43.　　Honours to devife.

The Edinburgh Folio Edit. reads more properly, " honours *deft* devife."

　　　　　　　　　　　　　　　The

The exclamation in the laſt line of this piece is particularly in Drui
mond's beſt manner.

Page 44. Sylveſter inſcribes a Hymn, " To the worthy friend of wo
thineſſe, Sir Peter Manwood, Knight of the Honourable order of the Bat
The father probably of Browne's friend.   561 p. Fol. Edit.

> Againſt the broad ſpread oke
> Each wind in furie bears ;
> *Yet fell their leaves not halfe ſo faſt*
> *As did the Shepheard's teares.*

In mere uncmpaſſioned deſcription, Similies which are derived from i
reign and remote objects, are frequently uſed with ſucceſs; for at the ſam
time that they afford the writer an opportunity of ſhewing his knowledg
they enrich and add a variety to Poetry, that it might not have attained by a
other means. Yet in pathetic ſituations when they immediately ariſe from t
ſubject itſelf, or ſome collateral branch of it, they conveigh the moſt direct a
unequivocal illuſtration with a conciſeneſs and expreſſion truly admirab
But how frequent is the practice, even with our beſt writers, in ſituations t
moſt pathetic, and in narratives the moſt urgent and intereſting, cooly
take leave of their ſubject, for the ſake of introducing a compariſon of pe
haps ten or twelve lines! The conſequence is, that our former ſympat
is thoroughly deſtroyed, and after toiling through the lines in queſtion, v
are left to recall our attention, aſſociate our diſtracted ideas, and recov
the loſt tone of our feelings at our leiſure, which is by this time moſt pr
bably totally out of our power. In ſuch caſes, a Simile taken from t
ground of the piece, (if I may be allowed the expreſſion) by confining o
attention wholly to the ſubject, and by giving us what we want, witha
obliging us to wander in queſt of it, would in three words, almoſt ha
completely anſwered the end of the Poet. I will ſubjoin an inſtance
two of this comprehenſive kind of illuſtration. Mallet thus deſcribes t
father of Edwin :

> The Father too, a ſordid man,
> Who love nor pity knew,
> *Was all unfeeling as the clod,*
> *From whence his riches grew.*
>
> Edw. and Emma.

Above all others perhaps Collins affords one of the moſt beautiful ſpe
mens, in lines that few have read without emotion.   Zara exclaims,

> " Farewell the Youth whom ſighs could not detain,
> Whom Zara's breaking heart implor'd in vain l
> Yet as thou go'ſt may ev'ry blaſt ariſe
> *Weak and unfelt as theſe rejected ſighs !*
> Safe o'er the wild, no perils may'ſt thou ſee,
> No griefs endure, nor weep, falſe youth, like me."
>
> Eclog. 2.

Broke was his tunefull pipe
That charm'd the chriftall floods.

Thus Milton, in the fineft vein of Poetry :

Thyrfis ! whofe artful ftrains have oft delay'd
The huddling brook to hear his madrigal.   494 Comus.

Page 46.   ——— —— and violets
For forrow hang their heads.

Milton, inftead of reprefenting the vegetable creation as affected at the
death of his friend, with fuperior judgement, calls for the feveral flowers,

" To ftrow the laureat herfe where Lycid lies."

Among which he mentions,

The glowing violet,
The mufk-rofe, and the well attir'd wood-bine,
With cowflips wan that hang the penfive head, &c.   145.

Milton, is fanciful, yet affecting ; Browne, puerile and difgufting.

Page 51.   Did he attend the court for no man's fall ?
Wore he the ruine of no Hofpitall ?
And when he did his rich apparell don,
Put be no widow, nor an orphan on ?

The moft finifhed character of Deteftation we have, is Maffinger's Sir
Giles Overreach. The following part of a dialogue will give the reader
fome infight into his exquifite talents for mifch ef.

Lovell. Are you not frighted with the imprecations and curfes of
whole families, made wretched by your finifter practices ?

Overreach. Yes, as rocks are,
When foamy billows fplit themfelves againft
Their flinty ribs ; or as the moon is mov'd,
When wolves, with hunger pin'd, howl at their brightnefs.
I'm of a folid temper, and like thefe
Steer on a conftant courfe, with mine own fword,
If call d into the field, I can make that right,
Which fearful eremies murmured at as wrong.
Now, for thofe other piddling complaints
Breath'd out in bitternefs ; as when they call me
Extortioner, Tyrant, Cormorant, or Intruder
On my poor neighbour's right ; or grand Inclofer
Of what was common, to my private ufe ;
Nay, when my ears are pierc'd with widows cries,
And undone orphans wafh with tears my threfhold ;
I only think what 'tis to have my daughter
Right honourable ; and 'tis a powerful charm
Makes me infenfible of remorfe or pity,
Or the leaft fting of confcience.
New way to pay Old Debts. Act. 4. Se. 1.

In

In the laſt Scene of the ſame Play, the diſtreſſes that he had occaſioned take faſt hold of his conſcience, and give riſe to the following terribly ſublime exclamation :

> " Ill fall to execution—ha ! I am feeble:
> *Some undone widow ſits upon mine arm.*
> *And takes away the uſe of 't ; and my ſword*
> *Glued to my ſcabbard with wrong'd orphans tears*
> *Will not be drawn,* &c.

Page 54. In this little Piece, of five lines only, there is a certain Greekneſs (if I may be allowed the expreſſion) that will not fail of captivating every reader of true taſte. We may juſtly apply on this occaſion a ſentence of Dryden, who ſays, " The ſweeteſt eſſences are always confined in the ſmalleſt glaſſes." Dedication to his Æneid :

> And in his *wrinkled* hand.

What a degree of animation and life is often thrown into a line by a ſingle pictureſque, and natural epithet ! In this reſpect Shakſpeare leaves all other poets far behind. To inſtance only in a ſingle paſſage. Henry the 5th, in his prayer before the battle of Agincourt, ſays,

> Five hundred poor I have in yearly pay
> Who twice a day their *wither'd* hands hold up
> Toward Heaven to pardon blood.   S. 5. 4 A.

Alter the epithet *wither'd* to almoſt any other, and you inſtantly deſtroy the picture ; for an epithet equally ſtriking, ſee Vol. 18. p.   . Applied to Old Age :

> His *wither'd* fiſt ſtill knocking at Death's dore.

Page 55.   Methinks, I hear a voice, &c.

There is an alarming ſolemnity in the concluſion of theſe lines, that reminds us of Tickell's juſtly popular Ballad :

> I hear a voice, you cannot hear,
> Which ſays I muſt not ſtay, &c.   Lucy and Collin.

Page 56.   ————— for if thy yeares
> Be number'd by thy virtues and our teares; &c.

Methuſalems may die at twenty-one. YOUNG.

Page 63.   ———— *deſtinate* to die.

One would ſuppoſe it ſhould be *deſtined.*

Page 66.   Inſtead of writing only rave in verſe.

This is what Pope calls, " rhyming with all the rage of impotence." 612. Eſſay on Chriticiſm.

Page 67.   Things common thou fpeak'ft proper.

A very difficult branch of the art to manage with dexterity, which Horace
has remark'd:

Difficile eft proprie communia dicere.   128. De Art. Poet.

That life, *That venus of all things——*

Probably immediately taken from Horace.

Ordinis hæc virtus erit *et venus.*   42. De Art. Poet.

Page 68.   As he who when he faw the ferpent wreath'd, &c.

The name of the archer here alluded to is Alcon. The following is
Servius' note in a folio edit. of Virgil, printed at Paris, 1500. See Eclog 11.
v. " Aicon is Cretenfis eft Sagittarius: et cum draco ejus puerum com-
plexus eft, adeo fuâ arte temperavit ictum fagittæ, ut in dracone transfixo
confifteret, neque ad puerum perveniret." According to the common
Delphin edition, the child's name was Fhaleris—but this ftory cannot, without the utmoft abfurdity, be applied to the fhepherd in Virgil, called Alcon, which, without doubt, was a common-place proper name for a paf-
toral character. See an Epigram on this ftory in Brunk's Analecta, vol.
i. p. 167.

—— the age grows more unfound
From the fool's balfam, than the wifeman's wound.
See Pope's Effay on Criticifm, from line 575 to 580.

Page 69.   Low without creeping, &c.

Thus Denham in his popular lines, addreffing the Thames:

O could I flow like thee ! and make thy ftream
My great example, as it is my theme;
Tho' deep yet clear; tho' gentle, yet not dull;
Strong, without rage ; without overflowing, full.
                                        Cooper's Hill.
See an excellent parody of thefe lines in the Dunciad. B. iii. 169.

Page 71.   There is a mafculine flow of good fenfe in this panegyric that
places Cartwright very high both as a poet and a critic. It appeared firft
in the Virbius: or The Memorie of Ben Johnfon revived by the Friends of
the Mufes, Lond. 1638. The verfes without a fignature, page 27, are
very excellent: they are alfo to be found in the Mifcellaneous Pieces fub-
joined to Cleiveland's Poems, p. 80. Lond. 1668.

Page 75. It were difficult to produce, from the whole mafs of Davenant's
poetry, fourteen fucceffive lines of fuch eafe and uninterrupted fweetnefs
of flow. Pope feems to have been fully fenfible of their merit:

Smooth as the face of waters firft appear'd, &c.
Still as the fea, ere winds were taught to blow. POPE.
Kind as the willing faints, *and calmer far*
Than in their fleeps forgiven hermits are. DAV.

Thus Pope. *Soft as the flumbers of a faint forgiven.* Eloifa.

Dave-

Davenant feems to have been fond of this idea, he has it again in his Condibert :

Calm as forgiven faints at their laft hour.   Cant. VIII.

Page 76.   Oft fhrouds his golden flame in likeft hair.

Randolph in fome humorous verfes, infcribed " To his well timbred Miftreffe," gives the following directions :

> Then place the garret of her head above,
> *That cht with a yellow hair to keep in love.*   p. 126. Ed. 1643.

Page 80.   Thefe verfes are fomewhat on the plan of Taffo's Amore fug-gitivo, who was indebted to the firft Idyllium of Mofchus. See an elegant paraphrafe of this in Crafhaw's " Delights of the Mufes," p. 110. Ed. 1670. Likewife the " Hue and Cry after Cupid," by Ben Jonfon, in his Mafque on the Marriage of Lord Hadington.

Page 82.   *Her watrie eyes* have burning force.

Anacreon, in his directions to the painter, orders him to give his miftrefs the *moift, watrie* eye :

> Τὸ δὲ βλίμμα νῦν ἀληθῶς
> Ἀπὸ τῦ πυρὸς πᾴησον
> Ἅμα γλαυκὶν, ὡς Ἀθήνῃς,
> Ἅμα δ᾽ ὑγρὸν, ὡς Κυθήρῃς.   In Amicam Suam.

> Her eye in filence hath a fpeach,
> Which eye beft underftands.

The expreffion of filence was never more poetically introduced, or applied with greater truth, than by Mr. Sheridan in his noble verfes to the memory of Garrick.

> Th' expreffive glance, whofe fubtile comment draws
> Entranc'd affection, and a mute applaufe ;
> Gefture that marks, with force and feeling fraught ;
> *A fenfe in filence*, and a will in thought.

G. Fletcher has, in his defcription of Juftice, with great fublimity, at-tributed to her the power of interpreting the filence of thought.

> ———— for fhe each wifh could find
> Within the folid heart ; and with her ears
> *The filence of the thought*, loud fpeaking hears.   Part I. St. 10.

The three little pieces by R. Southwell, which I have printed, were firft brought forward to the notice of general readers of poetry, by the editor of Ben Jonfon's Sad Shepherd, in his notes, from whence I have taken the liberty of extracting them. Obligations of this kind are but too commonly, to the difgrace of literature, very induftrioufly and ungratefully fuppreffed.

Page 85.   If thefe lines are genuine, they are extremely curious, as pre-fenting us with a lively picture of the workings of a great mind on an interefting

terefting occafion; and they ferve to afcertain a fact which does not appear to have been much noticed by hiftorians, that an habitual intercourfe of three months was not without its effect, and that the Queen felt ftrong emotions of regret for that denial, which fhe was perhaps under the neceffity of giving, in order to fatisfy her fubjects. From a manufcript in the Afhmolean Mufeum, the lines are tranfcribed; whether they have previoufly appeared in print, I know not: I am willing to believe them original, from internal evidence, yet I cannot perfectly diveft myfelf of fufpicion. Unfortunately the moft material word in the MS. is illegible; for after the fignature of *Eliza Regina*, the following words, informing us of the fubject on which the verfes were written, occurs. " Upon *Moun---s departure*," the word *Moun---s* being half obliterated. On my firft infpection of them, I had conceived they might have been compofed on Elizabeth's quarrel with Effex, who, of all her favourites, attracted moft of her perfonal affection, perhaps on his departure for his command in Ireland: but upon looking over Stow's account of the Duke of Alencon's vifit to England, I have had reafon to alter my opinion, as I think I have difcovered the real origin of the verfes, and believe the obliterated word in the MS. to be *Monfieur*.

Stow's account is as follows: " Thefe Lords (the Ambaffadors from France) after divers fecret conferences amongft themfelves, and returne of fundry letters into France, fignifying the Queenes declination from marriage, and the peoples unwillingnefs to match that way, held it moft convenient, that the Duke fhould come in proper perfon, whofe prefence they thought in fuch affaires might prevaile more than all their oratory: and thereupon, the firft of November, the fayd Prince came over in perfon, very princely accompanied, and attended, though not in fuch glorious manner as were the above named commiffioners, whofe entertainment, in all refpects, was equivalent unto his eftate and dignity. By this time his picture, ftate, and titles, were advanced in every ftationer's fhop, and many other publique places, by the name of *Fraunc:s* of *Valois*, Duke of *Alanfon*, heire apparent of France, and brother to the French King: but he was better knowne by the name of *Monfieur*, unto all forts of people, than by all his other titles. During his abode in England, he ufed all princely meanes to prefer his fuite, and in his carriage demeaned himfelfe like a true borne prince, and the heire of Fraunce: and when hee had well obferved the Queene's full determination, to continue a fingle life, hee pacified himfelfe, admiring her rare vertues and high perfections. * * * * * * * * * * * *. The Queene in all refpects fhewed as great kindneffe unto the Duke, and all his retinew, at their departure, as at any time before, and for period of her princely favours, in that behalfe, fhee, with great ftate, accompanied the Duke in perfon to Canterburie: where fhe feafted him and all his traine very royally, and then returned. The next day being the fixt of February, the Duke, with his French Lords and others, imbarked at Sandwich, &c.———— Annales 690 p. Ed. 1631.

Their marriage articles were drawn up, as may be feen in Camden's Annals, p. 372. Hearne's edit. The fame writer alfo mentions a very clofe intimacy as fubfifting between them. " Vis pudici amoris inter amatoria colloquia eò provexerit, ut annulum fuo digito detractum *Andini* (Anjou, one of his titles) impofuerit, certis quibufdam legibus inter ipfos adhibitis." 375, page. As dead Queens rank but with meaner mortals, we

may

may affert without much fear of contradiction, that little elfe can now be gratified by the perufal of Elizabeth's poetry, than mere curiofity. Her pretenfions to notice on this head are pretty much on a par with her pretenfions to beauty. Yet in both thefe fubjects, flender as they were, the poets and the courtiers of her age found fources for panegyric the moft inexhauftible.

Spencer concludes his " Tears of the Mufes" with a compliment to her in her poetical character, where he calls her a peerlefs poetefs. And in his Colin Clout, he fays of her,

> Whofe grace was great, and bounty moft rewardful
> Befides her peerlefs fkill in *making well*.

An other Poet of her age, has hazarded a very fingular compliment in the following lines :

> She with the feed of Jove, the Mufes nine,
> So frequent was in her yeares youthful prime,
> That fhe of them had learned power divine
> To quell proud love, if love at any time
> In her pure breft aloft began to clime.

England's Eliza, by R. Niccols, Edit. 1610.

If we may credit an old finner of antiquity on this fubject, the poets are the very laft teachers of abftinence; hear Ovid, who may be fairly fuppofed to have had fome little experience in thefe matters:

> Eloquar invitus : teneros ne tange Poetas,
> Submoveo dotes impius ipfe meas.   Rem. Amor. 727.

Page 90.   Muft learn the hateful art how to forget.

Thus Pope:

> Of all affliction taught a lover yet,
> 'Tis fure the hardeft fcience to forget. Eloifa.

Page 93.   This little piece is worth all the unmanly fniveling Elegies that Hammond ever wrote.

Page 95.   Thefe lines, though far from excellent, are ftill, in my opinion, better than any thing Sylvefter could have produced. I am therefore inclined to fufpect that the publifher of the Folio Edit. of Du Bartas in 1641, is miftaken in giving this to Sylvefter. In the fame Edit. p. 652, verfes entituled, " The Soules Errand," are to be found (printed in the 2d Vol of Dr. Percy's Reliques, under the title of " The Lye,") and beyond a doubt not his.

Page 97.   ———— gracing grace —⊸

This is a fort of Græcifm, as innumerable inftances of this form of expreffion will immediately fuggeft themfelves to the claffical reader, one inftance will be fufficient here :

—— hunc, oro, fine me *furere* ante *furorem*.

Virg. 12. Æn. 680.

Page 99. With loving *Red-breaft*.

This bird has juftly been a favourite with fome of our moft diftinguifhed poets, and has received due attention from them in their writings.
I will fet before the reader a few inftances, out of many which I have col-
lefted, perhaps rather too idly and unneceffarily. In a concert of birds by
Browne, Song 3. B. 1. the Red-breaft is thus diftinguifhed :

> The mounting larke, daie's herauld, got on wing
> Bidding each bird chufe out his bow and fing.
> The lofty treble fung the little wren;
> *Robin* the meane, *that beft of all loves men.*   Thomp. Edit.

In Nicolls's Cuckow, p. 12. Edit. 1607. in a collection of birds we meet
with

> The *Red-breaft* fweet, *that loves the looks of men.*

M. Drayton in his Owl :

> Covering with mofs the dead's unclofed eye
> The little *Red-breaft* teacheth charity.

Collins in his Dirge :

> The *Red-breaft* oft at evening hours
> Shall kindly lend his little aid
> With hoary mofs and gather'd flowers,
> To deck the ground where thou art laid.

But above all others on this fubject, Thomfon is intitled to fuperlative
praife :

> ——————————— one alone,
> The *Red-breaft*, facred to the houfehold Gods,
> Wifely regardful of th' embroiling fky,
> In joylefs fields, and thorny thickets, leaves
> His fhivering mates, and pays to trufted man
> His annual vifit. Half afraid, he firft
> Againft the window beats; then brifk, alights
> On the warm hearth; then, hopping o'er the floor,
> Eyes all the fmiling family afkance,
> And pecks, and ftarts, and wonders where he is;
> Till more familiar grown, the table-crumbs
> Attract his flender feet.   246. Winter.

See likewife a Stanza publifhed by Mr. Mafon, and originally intended by
Gray to have been introduced into his Elegy :

There

There-fcatter'd oft, the earlieft of the year
By hands unfeen are fhow'rs of violets found;
The *Red-breaft* loves to build and warble there,
And little footfteps lightly print the ground.

Page 100.   ———— *grim-grinning* King.

Milton I believe has been juftly and univerfally confidered as unrivalled, where he fays of Death, that he

Grinn'd horribly a ghaftly fmile.

I cannot refift the opportunity of fetting before my readers, a paffage, which though diffimilar in its fubject, and inferior in its merit, yet eminently well expreffes that mixture of contrary paffions which is frequently fublime. I have always confidered this inftance, as approaching nearer to the manner of Milton, than any thing I have met with in the whole courfe of my poetical reading. I the Mafque of the Gods, introduced in the Argalus and Parthenia of Quarles, the Goddeffe of the night is thus fancifully habited:

———————— her body was confinde
Within a coale-blacke mantle, thorow linde
With * fable furrs; her treffes were of hew
Like ebony, on which a perly dewe
Hung, like a fpiders web; her face did throw'd
A fwarth complexion, underneath a cloud
Of blacke curl'd cypreffe: on her head, fhe wore
A crowne of burnifht gold, befhaded o'er
With foggs and rory † mift; her hand did beare
A fcepter and a fable hemifphere;
She fternly fhook her dewy locks, and brake
A melancholy fmile, ————   B. 3. p. 112.

For this mixture of oppofite paffions, fee Spence on the Odyffey, p. 77, a truly claffical work, by no means fo popular as it fhould be, and to which we may well apply what Dr. Johnfon has afferted of Watts's Improvement of the mind, " Whoever has the care of inftructing others, may be charged with deficience in his duty, if this book is not recommended." See alfo Dr.

———

* Milton has arrayed Night in fables;

———— with him enthron'd
Sat *fable-vefted* Night—   2 B. 962. P. Loft.

† *Rory,* this word feems very undefervedly difufed. Fairfax has it in his Taffo:

And fhook his wings with *roary* may-dews wet.

Henry

Henry More's Mift. of Godlinefs, B. 6. Ch. 5. who compares the pleafures of this life to the *grinning laughter of Gb-fts* &c.

Page 101. The Sir W. Alexander to whom this Sonnet is addreffed, was afterwards created Earl of Sterline. He wrote poetry, a lift of which is given by Mr. Pinkerton, in his Ancient Scotifh Poems, p. 121. He was a particular friend of our Drayton's, as fhould feem from the verfes of the latter on " Poets and Poefy." He there ftyles him,

> That man whofe name I ever would have known
> To ftand by mine, &c.

There is a fenfible little tract of his, entituled, " A cenfure of fome poets, Ancient and Modern," and addreffed to Drummond of Hawthorden, his intimate friend, preferved in the Edinb. Edit. of the latter, p. 159.

Page 102.   Summer's *honour.*

Honour is frequently ufed by our old Poets for beauty. The Latins ufed *bonos*, in the fame manner, for *pulchritudo.* As in Horace:

> Non femper idem floribus eft *bonos*
> Vernis.   11 Od. 2 B.

Page 104. On this fubject poets of all ages and nations have been very eloquent; fuffice it to fay, that Shakfpeare in his Henry the 4th, Part 2. Act 3. Sc. 1. has furpaffed every thing that has hitherto appeared on the fame fubject. And his admirers may fafely defy the moft bigoted and induftrious fcholars to produce from the collected works of all antiquity, an invocation of fuch tranfcendent merit:

> Since I am thine, O come, &c.

In the original fpirit of the Greek Epigram, the following lines are compofed, and, as I have been informed, were intended to have been placed under a ftatue of Somnus, in the garden of the late learned Mr. James Harris of Salifbury; it will be no derogation to their beauties, to compare them with the conclufion of Drummond's Sonnet:

> Ad Somnum.
>
> Somne veni, et quanquam certiffima mortis imago es,
>   Confortem cupio te tamen effe tori !
> Huc ades, haud abiture cito : nam fic fine vitâ
>   Vivere, quam fuave eft, fic fine morte mori !

It may be neceffary to inform fome readers, that they are written by the prefent Poet Laureat. In Popham's Selecta Poemata, p. 57. they occur, but they appear to have undergone a revifal confiderably for the better, in the copy from which I have printed them. A tranflation of them is to be found in the Gent. Mag. for March 1775, p. 144.

Page 105. Drayton has here in the compafs of fourteen lines only been very profufe of fine compound epithets. *Silver-fanded fhore, foul-fhrined faint,*

milk-

milk-white fwans, myrrh-breathing Zephyr, nectar-dropping fhowers, dew-impearled flowers:

———— Browne compliments Drayton as the Swain
" Who on the bankes of *Ancor* turn'd his pipe."
See B 1. Song 5. p. 179,

Page 106.   That faireft ftates have *fatall* nights and dayes:

Fatall, here means *deftin'd by the Fates,* like the word *fatalis* in Latin:

" Non licuit fines Italos, *fataliaque arva*
" Nec tecum Aufonium, quicumque eft, quærere Tybrim."
Æn. 5. 82.

Page 108.   —immelodious.   A word very harmonious and uncommon.
Milton ufes " ineloquent," 8 P. Loft. 219.

Page 109.   The fhipwreck of my ill-advifed youth.

He again fays,

" Look on the dear expences of my youth."   p. 111.

Lord Surry upbraids Beauty, and calls it

Enemy to youth, that moft may I bewaile.   p. 96.

Page 113.   Or moone at night in *jettie ebariot* roll'd ?

Browne reprefents night as drawn in a carriage of the fame materials:

All-drowfie Night, *who in a carre of jet*
By fteedes of iron-gray drawne through the fky.
Brit. Paft. B 2. Son. 1. p. 33. Th. Edit.

Page 114.   Where flave-born man playes to the fcoffing ftarres,

This language of defperation may be compared with thefe lines of Drayton :

＊ ＊ ＊ ＊ ＊ ＊ ＊
Which doth inforce me partly to prefer
The opinion of that mad Philofopher,
Who taught that thofe all-framing Powers above
(As 'tis fuppos'd) made man not out of love
To him at all, but only as a thing
To make them fport with, which they ufe to bring
As men do monkies, puppets, and fuch tools.
Drayton to W. Browne.

In contradiction to this abfurd and uncomfortable doctrine, let us hear
what one of the wifeft and greateft men this country has produced, fays,
" But that Nature fhould implant in man fuch a ftrong propenfion to religion, which is the reverence of a Deity, there being neither God nor Angel
nor

nor Spirit in the world, is such a slur committed by her as there can be in no wise excogitated any excuse for. If there were a higher species of things to laugh at as we do at the ape, it might seem more tolerable." Dr. H. More's Antidote against Atheism, 1655 Edit. p. 152. The concluding idea in this extract somewhat reminds us of a line in Pope's Essay on Man:

> Superior beings * * *
> * * * * * * *
> Admir'd such wisdom in an earthly shape
> *And shew'd a Newton as we shew an Ape.*

Page 115. Turn'st is here used for return'st.
Page 116. The best of Spenser's Sonnets is addressed to the Spring. See 5 Vol. p. 73 Hugh. Edit.

> And twice it is not given thee to be born.

A mere reference might disappoint the classical reader; as such I shall make no scruple to quote at length the well known beautiful lines of Moschus on this subject:

> Αἴ, Αἱ ταὶ μαλάχαι μὲν ἐπὰν κατὰ κᾶπον ὄλωνται,
> Η τα γλ ρα σίλινα, τὶ τ' εὐθαλὲ ὕλον ἀνηθον,
> Υσίερον αὖ ζωἡ τι καὶ εἰς ἔτος ἄλλο φύοντι·
> Αμμες δ' οἱ μι άλοι καὶ καρτερι ἢ σοφοὶ άνδρες
> Οππότε πρῶτα θάνωμες, ἀνάκοοι ἐν χθονὶ κοίλα
> Εὔδομες ὖ μάλα μακρὸν ἀτέρμονα νήγρετον ὕπνον.

I never saw the spirit of these verses better transfused, than in the following extract from the very early production of a friend, whose poetry is among the least of his many elegant attainments:

> Yet mark the violet, how it loads with sweets
> The pregnant gale, spreading its purple leaves,
> The painted pink too, with the rose-bud's bloom,
> And fair narcissus catch th' enchanted eye.
> When winter's frost arrests the rushing stream,
> And binds in icy chains the sadden'd year;
> Fled is their beauty, fled that fragrant breath
> Wont to regale the weary passenger.
> But when the spring etherial mildness sheds,
> And bids the brook its former flow resume,
> Up springs the lark, Aurora's messenger,
> Glad'ning the goat-herd with his early song,
> Each plant, each flower, inhales the genial breath,
> And opening into life, again pours forth,
> Loose on the zephyr, all its wonted sweets.
> Again the violet dark resumes its hue,
> Nor wanting to the rose-bud is its bloom.
> Whate'er amid the plant creation, erst
> Conspir'd to make the joyous year complete,

Again

Again fhoots forth, renewing all its power:
Then why boafts Man his origin divine,
(Lord of the Univerfe, Creation's pride)
His fpring but once, but once his winter comes
And when he falls, he falls to rife no more?

This note has been already too much extended to admit of Dr. Jortin's Imi-
tation of Mofchus's lines. See p. 32. Lufus Poet.

Page 117. The Ancients feem to have been equally attached to this
bird, as the Moderns Attentive mention is made of it in Homer, Theo-
critus, Virgil. and Horace, and Mr. Huntingford in his Apology for the
Monoftropl ics (one of the few controverfial works in which the fcholar
and the gentleman are moft happily blended,) has by many paffages proved
it the favourite alfo of Sophocles. See p. 89, &c. Some of the beft poets of
this country have figaified their partiality to it, in ftrains almoft as delicious as its own. Milton's regard for it muft be well known to all his
readers as it has been remarked by almoft all his commentators. Thomfon *,
pre eminently the Poet of Nature, who wrote immediately from obfervation, has not been wanting in its praifes. Gray has remembered it in his
Ode to the Spring. Is it not fomewhat ftrange that Collins fhould have
omitted to mention this bird? In all his poetry I recollect no allufion to this
fubject, and have always confidered the abfence of Philomel as no trivial
blemifh in his Ode to Evening. But above all the panegyrics that have been
defervedly paffed upon this univerfal favourite, I have feen nothing yet,
that in any degree approaches the notice of one who was certainly no poet;
my reader will be furprifed perhaps when I name honeft Izack Walton,
but let him read this and judge. " But the Nightingale, another of my airy
creatures, breathes fuch fweet loud mufick out of her little inftrumental
throat, that it might make mankind to think miracles are not ceafed. He
that at midnight, when the very labourer fleeps fecurely, fhould hear, as I
have very often, the clear airs, the fweet † *defcants*, the natural rifing and
falling, the doubling and redoubling of her voice, might well be lifted
above earth, and fay, " *Lord, what mufick haft thou provided for the Saints in
Heaven, when thou affordeft bad men fuch mufick on earth.*" Compl. Angler,
page 1.

---

* The elegant and ingenious Mr. Pennant, has very properly quoted in
his Britifh Zoology, every paffage from Milton in which it is mentioned.

† ——————The wakeful nightingale
She all night long her amorous *defcant* fung.

P. Loft 4 B. 603.

I will

I will fubjoin a few defcriptions from our older Poets. Niccols has been very minute on this head:

> The little Philomel with curious care
> *Setting* + *alone* her ditties did prepare,
> And many tunes, whofe harmonie did paffe
> All mufike elfe that ere invented was;
> One while the meane part fhe did fweetly warble,
> The tennor now, the bafe and then the treble:
> Then all at once with many parts in one
> Dividing fweetly in divifion;
> Now fome tweete ftraine to mind fhe doth reftore,
> Which all the winter fhee had conn'd before,
> And with fuch cunning *defkants* thereupon,
> That curious art ne'er doctrin'd any one
> With lute, with violl, or with voice in quire
> That to her matchleffe mufike might afpire.
>
>   The Cuckow, p. 12, 1607.

Bird-fanciers are accuftomed to call the practice of old birds teaching their young to fing, *recordin*; from this circum.tance Drayton very poetically and fancifully dates the origin of mufic, which I think exceeds what Lucretius has advanced on the fame fubject, Lib. 5. 1378 line.

> —————— Philomel in fpring
> Teaching by art her little one to fing;
> *By u .ife clear voice fweet mufic firft was found*
> *Before Amphion ever knew a found.*   The Owl.

Browne, a very minute obferver, and fometimes an accurate defcriber of Nature and rural objects, has remarked the fame property of this Bird:

> Under whofe fhade the Nightingale would bring
> Her chirping young, *and teach them how to fing.*
>
>   Brit. Paft. 1 B. 5 Song.

In mentioning the time before fun-rife, he introduces it again:

> For the Turtle and her mate
>   Sitten yet in neft:
> And the Thruftle hath not been
> Gath'ring wormes yet on the green,
>   But attends her reft.

——————————

* This is Thomfon's:

> ————— ———— on the bough
> *Sole-fitting.*   722. Spring,

                                             Not

Not a bird hath taught her young,
Nor her morning's leffon fung
  In the fhady grove ;
But the Nightingale *in dark* *
Singing, woke the mounting Larke
  She *records* her love.

                    Shepheard's Pipe. 3 Eclog.

But Browne attributes the cuftom of teaching, to other birds as well as the Nightingale, defcribing a place of retirement, he fays,

  Wherein melodious birds did nightly harbour :
  And on a bough, within the quickning fpring,
  Would be a teaching of their young to fing.   Song 3. B. 1.

See Andrew Marvel's " Appleton Houfe," who touches upon the Nightingale, p. 65. Vol. I. Cooke's Edit.
  Drayton defcribes with great fpirit a confort of birds, in which the Nightingale is highly diftinguifhed :

When Phœbus lifts his head out of the winter's wave,
No fooner doth the earth her flowery bofom wave,
At fuch time as the year brings on the pleafant fpring,
But hunts-up to the morn the feath'red fylvans fing :
And in the lower grove, as on the rifing knole,
Upon the higheft fpray of every mounting pole,
Thofe quirifters are perch't with many a fpeckled breaft.
Then from her burnifht gate the goodly glitt'ring Eaft
Gilds every lofty top, which late the humorous night
Befpangled had with pearl, to pleafe the morning's fight :
On which the mirthful quires, with their clear open throats,
Unto the joyful morn fo ftrain their warbling notes,
That hills and vallies ring, and even the echoing air
Seems all compos'd of founds, about them every where.
The Throftel, with fhrill fharps ; as purpofely he fong
T' awake the luftlefs fun ; or chiding, that fo long
He was in coming forth, that fhould the thicke s thrill :
The Woofel near at hand, that hath a golden bill :
As nature him had markt of purpofe, t' let us fee
That from all other birds his tunes fhould different be :
For, with their vocal founds, they fing to pleafant May ;
Upon his dulcet pipe the Merle doth only play.   `
When in the lower brake, the Nightingale hard-by,
In fuch lamenting ftrains the joyful hours doth ply,
As though the other birds fhe to her tunes would draw,
And, (but that Nature by her all-conftraining law)

          —————

* This is Milton's :

    —————as the wakeful bird
  Sings *darkling*———   38. B. 3. P. Loft.

                              Each

Each bird to her own kind this season doth invite,
They else, alone to hear that charmer of the night,
(The more to use their ears) their voices jure would spare,
That moduleth her tunes so admirably rare,
As man to set in parts at first had learn'd of her.

Poly-Olbion, 13 Song.

See likewise a very minute and accurate defcription in Sylvester's Du Bartas, p. 44 Fol. Edit. 1641. See p. 1319. 4. Vol. 1536 ibid. Drayton Oldy's Edition.

To accumulate yet more inftances, of a fimilar nature would be neither difficult nor unpleafing :

Sed fugit interea, fugit irreparabile tempus,
Singula dum capti circumvectamur amore. VIRG.

To him who has been " long in populous cities pent," who has feldom been accuftomed to view " each rural fight" with poetical eyes, and to " each rural found" has turn'd a deaf or an undelighted ear, thefe notices, it is feared, will feem moft diminutive and frivolous; but to others who have heard from this bird

———Strains that might create a foul
Under the ribs of Death,

in the luxurious groves of Hertfordfhire, it is hoped, however unimportant they may be, that they will at leaft be confidered as not incurious.

Page 118. ——— for weedes at Normandie by this in porches groe.

Meaning, that they had fo exhaufted their country (Normandy) by the forces they had draughted from it already, that its cities were left defolate and uninhabited. The expreffion is aukward ; but the idea is forcible, and not unlike what Thomfon fays of the effects of the plague :

Empty the ftreets, *with uncouth verdure clad;*
Into the wo' ft of defarts fudden turn'd
The chearful haunt of men.   Summer, 1060.

Page 119.   Yea pardon hath he to depart, &c.

Thus Henry the 5th to his foldiers :

——————— dont wifh one more :
Rather proclaim it (Weftmoreland) through my hoft,
That he which hath no ftomach to this fight,
Let him depart. SHAKSPEARE.

Page 120.   ——————— this is my ground or grave.
See the Speech of Alric in Claudian on invading Italy.

Hanc ego vel victor regno, vel morte tenebo
Victus humum.   De Bell. Gent. 530.

Page

Page 126.   And in the faces of their foes your women, in defpight,
Should fling their fuckling babes.

How exquifitely unnatural is a profeffion of lady Macbeth's in this way:

——— I have giv'n fuck, and know
How tender 'tis to love the babe that milks me,
I would, while it was fmiling in my face,
Have pluck't my nipple from his bonelefs gums
And dafht the brains out, had I but fo fworn
As you have done to this———

Page 125.   Her name is written indifferently Voadicea, Boodicea, Bunduica, and Bondicea.   Selden's Notes on Drayton.

Page 126.   ———Pichtes of Scythian breed.

Thofe who may be inclined to examine into the hiftory of this nation, are referred to a very mafterly enquiry, entituled, " A Differtation on the origin and progrefs of the Scythians or Goths," by the able and ingenious Mr. Pinkerton, lately publifhed.   To this Gentleman (if there is not an impertinence in the manner of my doing it,) I would recommend as a motto for many of his works the following verfe:

Πρὸς σοφίην μὲν ἔχειν τόλμαν, μάλα σύμφορόν ἐστι.
Poet Min. Græci. p. 515. 1635 Edit. Cantabrig.

Page 127.   For the circumftances of this interview, fee Livy 11. Lib. See alfo Plutarch's life of Publicola.

SUPPLEMENT.

SUPPLEMENT.

Notwithstanding the following incidental Remarks bear no relation to particular passages in the Extracts which compose these volumes, yet they are intimatey connected with some of the respective Authors from whom these Extracts are taken; and being in themselves both too foreign as well as too extensive for insertion in the course of the notes, it was thought necessary to give them a place here.

F. QUARLES.

In selecting from this author, I have been obliged to omit many of his beauties from their unfortunate intermixture with the most unpardonable vulgarisms; in gathering flowers from such soils, weeds will unavoidably obtrude themselves; in order however that the elegance and exactness of some of his similies, which were too short to be admitted into the body of the book, may not be overlooked, I take the opportunity of introducing them to the reader here, and should think that critic more fastidious than clear-sighted, who should be displeased with them.

> Even as the soyle (which April's gentle showers
> Have fild with sweetnesse, and enrich't with flowers)
> Reares up her suckling plants, still shooting forth
> The tender blossomes of her timely birth,
> But, if deny'd the beams of cheerly May,
> They hang their withered heads, and fade away;

Se

So man, affifted by th' Almightie's hand,
His faith doth flourifh and fecurely ftand,
But left awhile, forfooke (as in a fhade)
It languifhes, and nipt with fin doth fade.

          Joh. Millitant, Med. 6.

As when a lady (walking Flora's Bowre)
Picks here a pinke, and there a gilly-flowre,
Now plucks a vilet from her purple bed,
And then a primrofe (the yeeres maidenhead)
There, nips the bryer, here, the Lover's pauncy,
Shifting here dainty pleafures, with her fancy,
This, on her arme, and that, fhe lifts to weare
Upon the borders of her curious haire
At length, a rofe-bud (paffing all the reft)
She plucks, and bofomes in her lilly brefts.

          Hift. of Queene Efter, Sect. 6

Even as a Hen (whofe tender brood forfakes
The downy clofet of her wings, and takes
Each its affected way) markes how they feed,
This, on that crum, and that, on t' other feed,
Moves, as they move, and ftayes, when as they ftay,
And feems delighted in their infant-play :
Yet (fearing danger) with a bufie eye,
Lookes here and there if ought fhe can efpy
Which (unawares) might fnatch a booty from her,
Eyes all that paffe, and watches ev'ry commer;
Even fo the affection, &c.

          Job. Mil. Sect. 1.

Like as the *Haggard*, cloiftered in her mew,
To fcowr her downy robes, and to renew
Her broken flags, preparing t' overlook
The tim'rous mallard at her fliding brook,
Jets oft from perch to perch, from ftock to ground,
From ground to window, thus furveying round
Her dove-befeather'd prifon, 'till at length
Calling her noble birth to mind, and ftrength
Whereto her wing was born, her ragged beak
Nipps of her jangling * *jeffes*, ftrives to break
Her gingling fetters and begins to bate
At ev'ry glimpfe, and darts at ev'ry grate.

          Emb. 1. 3. B.

———

*   ——— If I prove her *baggard*,
Though that her *jeffes* were my dear heart ftrings
I'd whiftle her off, and let her down the wind
To prey at fortune.   OTHELLO.

                     Even

Even as the needle, that directs the howre,
(Toucht with the loadstone) by the secret power
Of hidden Nature, points upon the pole ;
Even so the wavering powers of my soule,
Toucht by the virtue of thy spirit, flee
From what is earth, and point alone to Thee.

Job. Mil. 4 Med.

In the beautiful song of " Sweet William's Farewell," the sailor with great propriety adopts a nautical term from his own Art :

Change as ye lift, ye winds ; my heart shall be
The faithful compass that still points to thee.

In perufing Quarles, I have occasionally obferved that he has fometimes taken thoughts from the works of Lord Sterline, but the paffages were hardly worth noticing. Quarles was indebted to Herman Hugo for the hint of writing Emblems, the earlieft edition I have been able to meet with, is that published in 1623 at Antwerp, in tolerable good Latin Elegies. A tranflation of it appeared Lond. 1686, by Edm. Arwaker, M. A. who very injudiciously obferves, that " Mr. Quarles only borrowed his Emblems, to prefix them to much *inferior* fenfe." The earlieft edition of Quarles's book, that I have feen, is in 1635, all the prints from the beginning of the third book, are exactly copied from Hugo, but Hugo himfelf was not original. As Andrew Alciat, a Milaneze lawyer fo early as 1535, publifhed at Paris a volume of Emblems. Thuanus gives a great character of this writer. Hift. Lib 8. A fmall Edit. of Alciat's work, with the obfervations of C. Minos, partially extracted, was publifhed at Geneva. There is a pretty thought in one of the emblems which confifts of a Helmet turned into a Beehive, and furrounded on all fides with its inhabitants, the motto is, *Ex bello pax*. I mention it folely to obferve, that in the Sonnet fung before Queen Elizabeth at a tilt in the year 1590 at Weftminfter, and fuppofed to have been compofed by the Earl of Effex, a thought of the fame kind occurs :

My helmet now fhall make an hive for bees,
And lovers fongs fhall turn to holy pfalmes, &c.

See Vol. III. Evans's Ballads.

The writer of the fame fong, whoever he was, might have been indebted for the thought to fome print of the kind.

W. WARNER.

Milton's commentators have omitted remarking, that in the following paffage he feems to have had an eye on Warner :

Thee bright-hair'd *Vefta* long of yore
To folitary Saturn bore ;
His daughter fhe, *in Saturns reign*
Such mixture was not held a ftain. Il Pens.

Thus

This in Albion's England:

> In Crete did florifh in thofe daies (firft there that flourifht fo)
> Uranos: he in wealth and wit all others did outgoe.
> This tooke to wife *(not then forbod)* his fifter *Vefta* fayre.

B. 1 Ch. 1.

    The turn of thinking in the following lines will remind the reader of Pope. Sir J. Mandeville during his travels, writes to Eleanor, the coufin of King Edward, who according to Warner's ftory had fallen in love with him. The following forms a part of the epiftle:

> Great ftore of beauties have I feene, but none as yours exact,
> Courts alfo more than ftatelie with faire ladies in the fame,
> Which feem'd but common forms to me, remembring but your
>   name.
> When in the holy-land I pray'd, even at the holy grave,
> *(Forgive me God): figh fr finne, and there for love i gave.*
> Againft the fierce Arabians I the Soldan's pay did take,
> *When of, as enjit, for Saint George Saint Eleanor I fpake.*

B. 10. Ch. 63.

    " Not on the crofs my eyes were fix'd but you."

Again:

    " Thy image fteals between my God and mee." ELOISA.

W. DRUMMOND.

    One would be almoft led to fuppofe that Pope had feen and remembered thefe lines:

> Ah! as a Pilgrime who the Alpes doth paffe,
> Or Atlas temples crown'd with winter's glaffe,
> The ayrie Caucafus, the Apennine,
> Pyrene's cliftes where funne doth never fhine,
> When he fome heapes of hilles hath overwent,
> Beginnes to think on reft, his journey fpent,
> Till mounting fome tall mountaine hee doe finde
> More hights before him thann he left behinde.

Drum. p. 38. 4to Edit.

> So pleas'd at firft the towring Alps we try,
> Mount o'er the vales, and feem to tread the fky,
> Th' eternal fnows appear already paft,
> And the firft clouds and mountains feem the laft;

But

But thofe attain'd, we tremble to furvey
The growing labour of the lengthen'd way,
Th' increafing profpect tires our wond'ring eyes,
Hills peep o'er hills, and Alps on Alps arife!

Effay on Crit. 228.

The following lines, defcribing God moved to wrath, are in Milton's
manner:

So feeing Earth, of Angels once the inn,
Manfion of Saints, deflowred all by fin,
And quite confus'd, by wretches here beneath;
The World's great Sovereign moved was to wrath,
Thrice did he rowfe himfelf, thrice from his face
Flames fparkle did throughout the heavenly place.
The ftars, though fixed, in their rounds did quake;
The earth, and earth-embracing fea, did fhake:
Carmel and Hæmus felt it, Athos tops,
Affrighted fhrunk, and near the Æthiops
Atlas, the Pyrenees, the Appennine,
And lofty Grampius, which with fnow doth fhine.
Then to the Synod of the Sp'rits he fwore,
Man's care fhould end, and time fhould be no more;
By his own felf he fwore ——, &c.

Poems, p. 33. Edin. Ed. 1711.

The beft of Drummond's profe works, is his " Cyprefs Grove," which
though quaint in its ftyle, is worth reading for its vein of dignified morality.
Mr. Pinkerton, in his lift of Scotch Poets, calls it " a poor piece of tinfel,"
and fays of its author, that " like other great poets, he could not write
profe." I will venture to affert, that he is more miftaken in his general
pofition, than even in the particular inftance fpecified. Many of our beft
poets have rivalled, and fome have exceeded the profeffional profe-writers
of their day. We have no contemporary piece of profe to compare in
purity with Spenfer's "View of the ftate of Ireland," or even with Daniel's
" Apology for Rhyme." Cowley was unrivalled by any profe-writer;
Davenant's Preface to his Gondibert, is a good piece of nervous writing. Are
Dryden's fine Prefaces to be forgotten, or Pope's Letters and Preface to his
works, one of the moft polifhed pieces we have? but above all, the profe
of Goldfmith is the ftrongeft contradiction of his affertion, it is the model
of perfection, and the ftandard of our language, to equal which the efforts of
moft would be vain; and to exceed it every expectation, fully.

P. FLETCHER.

At the bright lamp of Spenfer, who's flame will never expire but with our language, many inferior bards have lighted their flender torches. The perufal of the Fairy Queen, biaffed the minds both of Cowley and More * to the purfuit of poetry. And to them we may add Fletcher, who not contented with deriving his general tafte for Allegory and Perfonification from him, has gone fo far as immediately to adopt imagery and particular figures. Though it may fomewhat detract from the invention of Fletcher to compare him in fome inftances with his original, yet it is the only method of forming a real eftimate of his merits; and as Dr. Johnfon well obferves, " it is the bufinefs of critical juftice to give every bird of the Mufes his proper feather;" nor has he himfelf been backward in due acknowledgement, as thefe inftances fufficiently evince :

> Two Shepherds moft I love with juft adoring ;
> That Mantuan fwain, who chang'd his flender reed
> To trumpets martiall voice, and warres loud roaring,
> From Corydon to Turnus derring deed;
> *And next our home-bred Colins fweeteft firing ;*
> *Their fteps not following clofe, but farre admiring :*
> *To lackey one of thefe is all my pride's afpiring.*
>
> Can. 6. 5 St. P. III.

The following Eulogium to his memory does equal credit to his heart as to his abilities, and deferves being brought forward to notice. He is lamenting the fate of Genius :

> Witneffe our *Colin* † ; whom though all the graces,
> And all the Mufes nurft ; whofe well taught fong
> Parnaffus felf, and Glorian ‡ embraces,
> And all the learn'd, and all the fhepherds throng ;
> Yet all his hopes were croft, all fuits deni'd ;
> Difcourag'd, fcorn'd, his writings vilifi'd :
> Poorly (poore man) he liv'd; poorly (poore man) he di'd.

> And had not that great Hart §, (whofe honour'd head
> Ah lies full low) piti'd thy wofull plight;
> There hadft thou li'en unwept, unburied,
> Unbleft, nor grac't with any common rite :
> Yet fhalt thou live, when thy great foe || fhall fink
> Beneath his mountain tombe, whofe fame fhall ftink ;
> And time his blacker name fhall blurre with blackeft ink.

---

* Preface to his Philofophical Poems, 1647. Edit. † Spenfer.
‡ Elizabeth.   § Earl of Effex. || Burleigh.

O let th' Iambic Mufe revenge that wrong,
Which cannot flumber in thy fheets of lead:
Let thy abufed honour crie as long
As there be quills to write, or eyes to reade:
   On his ranke name let thine own notes be turn'd,
  " *Oh may that man that hath the Mufes fcorn'd,*
Alive, nor dead, be ever of a Mufe adorn'd!"

Can. 1. St. 19. &c.

He again touches on the misfortune of Spenfer Can. 6. St. 52.

But to come more immediately to the feveral parallel paffages, let the reader compare Fletcher's *Gluttonie.* Can. 7. Stan 80. with Spenfer's B. 1. Can. 4. 21 and 22 Stan. F. Queen. compare Fletcher's *Atimus.* Cant. 8. 42 Stan. &c. with Spenfer's *Idlenefs.* B. 1. 4 Cant. St. 18. compare Fletcher's *Thumos.* Can. 7. St. 55. with Spenfer's *Wrath.* B. 1. Can. 4. St. 33. compare Fletcher's *Afelges.* Can. 7. St. 23. with Spenfer's *Lechery.* B. 1. Can. 4. St. 24. compare Fletcher's *Pleconektes.* Can. 8. Stan. 24. with Spenfer's *Avarice.* B. 1. Can. 4. St. 27. compare Fletcher's *Envie.* Can. 7. St. 66. with Spenfer's *Envy.* B. 1. Can. 4. St. 30. likewife with another defcription. B. 5. Can. 12. St. 31. Some of Fletcher's lines well exprefs what Pope with great felicity ftyles, " *daming with faint praife.*"

> When needs he muft, yet faintly, then he praifes;
> Somewhat the deed, much more the means he raifes:
> So marreth what he makes, and praifing moft, difpraifes.

Compare Fletcher's *Deilos.* Can. 8. St. 10. with Spenfer's *Fear.* B. 3. Can. 12. St. 12. There feems to me more nature and real poetry in Fletcher's defcribing him as but *ftarting* at the fight of his arms, than in Spenfer. who on the fame occafion reprefents him as abfolutely " *flying faft away,*" but perhaps Speafer has hightened the image by making him equally terrified with the *found* of them as the *fight*; this is omitted in Fletcher. No one of Fletcher's figures is more confiftently habited, than his *Death.*

> A dead man's fkull fuppli'd his helmet's place,
> A bone his club, his armour fheets of lead:
> Some more, fome leffe fear his *all-frighting* face;
> But moft who fleep in downie pleafures bed.   12 Can. 38.

Yet the firft of thefe terrific attributes is fuggefted by Spenfer, who has given it to Meleager:

> Upon his head he wore an helmet light,
> Made of a dead man's fkull, that feem'd a ghaftly fight.

11 B. 11 Can. St. 22.

In the preceding part of this Canto of Spenfer, in which the foes of Temperance befiege her dwelling place, we find fight, hearing, fmell, and tafte, perfonified, which remind us of Fletcher, and difgrace Spenfer. I have often thought that a painter of tafte might extract from the Purple Ifland, a feries of Allegorical Figures, which if well executed might do honour to his pencil; though in fome inftances he would find Fletcher "nimis Poeta," in others he

would

would have little to do but to fupply the colours: and as there can be no ne-ceffity for implicitly tying him down to his original, the liberty of rejecting fuperfluities, and fupplying deficiencies fhould be allowed. The motto's and impreffes, which in general are very happily adapted, give Fletcher's figures an air of life, which in that particular renders them fuperior to thofe of Spenfer and of Sackville *. The following rich figure of Hope (which is re-prefented as Mafculine,) is among Fletcher's beft pieces, the attitude of his leaning on his attendant Pollicita, to whom every female grace might be given, feems worth/ the notice of a painter. I will quote the defcription at length, as it affords me an opportunity of comparing it with a figure of Spenfer on the fame fubject :

Next went *Elpinus*, clad in † *fky-like* blue ;
And thro' his arms few ftars did feem to peep,
Which there the workman s hand fo finely drew,
That rock'd in clouds they foftly feem'd to fleep :
   His rugged fhield was like a rockie mold,
   On which an anchour bit with fureft hold :
I hold by being held, was written round in gold.

Nothing fo cheerfull was his thoughtfull face,
As was his brother Fido's : fear feem'd dwell
Clofe by his heart ; his colour chang'd apace,
And went, and came, that fure all was not well :
   Therefore a comely Maid did oft fuftain
   His fainting fteps, and fleeting life maintain :
Pollicita fhe hight, which ne'er could lie or feigne.

Can. 9. St 30.

---

* Æfchylus in his " Seven againft Thebes" has fhewn much fancy in the mottos and devices of the fhields of the different chiefs.

† Pyracles in Sidney's Arcadia, is dreffed in a garment of the fame ma-terials, " Upon her body fhe wore a doublet of *fky-colour* fatin," &c. p. 42. Milton alfo has his " *fky-tinctured grain*," P. L. B. 5. 285. but Fletcher might have had a paffage in Quarles in his eye, who after defcribing Parthenia in a robe befpangled with ftars of gold, adds,

——————— her difhevel'd haire
Hung loofely downe, and vayl'd the backer part
Of thofe her *fkie-refembling robes*; but fo,
That every breath would wave it to and fro,
Like flying clouds, through which you might difcover
Sometimes one glim'ring ftarre, fometimes another.

B. 111. Arg. and Par.

The

The following is Spenſer's perſonification which is delineated with greater chaſtity than uſual:

> With him went Hope in rank, a handſome maid,
> Of chearful look and lovely to behold;
> In ſilken ſamite ſhe was light array'd,
> And her fair locks were woven up in gold:
> She always ſmil'd, and in her hand did hold
> An holy-water ſprinkle, dipt in dew,
> With which ſhe ſprinkle'd favours manifold,
> On whom ſhe liſt, and did great liking ſhew;
> Great liking unto many, but true love to few.

B. 3. Can. 12. St. 13.

This figure is ſimple, and the attributes new; Hope is here diveſted of her uſual emblem, the anchor, (which Fletcher has preſerved,) and the water-ſprinkle ſubſtituted in its room, which gives a religious air to the image; had it but received the ſanction of antiquity for its adoption, we might perhaps have heard more in its praiſe. On their coins, the Ancients we find repreſented Hope in the character of a ſprightly girl looking forward and holding a bloſſom, or bud in her right hand *, whilſt with her left, ſhe holds up her garment to prevent its retarding her pace. On a coin of Hadrian, I have ſeen Fortune and Hope with this emblem. Mr. Spence has juſtly objected againſt Spenſer, that many of his Allegorical Perſonifications are inconſiſtent, complicated, and overdone; he obſerves, that when they are well-invented, they are not well-marked out, and inſtances amongſt others the figure of Hope now before us. But ſurely though his general charge may be true, in this inſtance he has been miſled by his claſſical taſte, and too great a reverence for the Ancients; to expect an implicit adherence to them in all their mythological appendages, is unreaſonable and abſurd, and at once puts a ſtop to every exertion of fancy and genius; it is but doing juſtice to them to acknowledge that their emblematic figures are unrivaled, but as their ſeveral diſtinct attributes are cloſely connected with, and indeed drawn from their religion, hiſtory, dreſs, and manners, they muſt be conſidered as relatively excellent only; we cannot be ſo barren of invention, as to be obliged tamely to have recourſe to their imagery on all occaſions; the religion, hiſtory, manners, and dreſs, of our own country, are ſufficiently dignified to ſupply a fertile imagination, with combinations infinitely new, and to juſtify us in forming a ſtyle of our own. Propriety in ſelection is every thing; to produce a ſtrong effect from a few maſterly outlines, and to give an individual and excluſive character to the perſonage, ſeems to have been the ſole aim of the Ancients; from the profuſion of ornaments with which moſt modern allegorical figures are overwhelmed, we are as much at a loſs to diſcover for whom they are deſigned, as we are to unravel a rebus or an anagram. Milton appears to have been a reader of Fletcher. I will conclude theſe deſultory remarks on him, with noticing a few paſ-

---

* We commonly ſay, " to deſtroy our bopes in the bud."

ſages

fages that have efcaped the commentators of our Divine Bard. `Milton is invoking *Mirth* to bring with her,

> Nods and becks, and wreathed *fmiles,*
> Such as hang on Hebe's cheek,
> And love to live in dimple fleek ;
> *Sport* that *wrinkled Care defides,*
> And *Laughter* holding both his fides.
>
> L'Alleg. 28.

When this exquifite affemblage was formed, it is more than probable, that the poet had an eye on the following paffage of Fletcher :

> Here *fportfull* Laughter dwells, here ever fitting,
> *Defies* all lumpifh griefs, *and wrinkled care*;
> And twentie merrie mates *mirth* caufes fitting,
> And *fmiles,* which *Laughter's* fonnes, yet infants are.
>
> P. Ifland. Can. 4. St. 13. Edit. 1633.

> Where thou perhaps under the *whelming* tide.
>
> Lycid. 157.

In the Edit of 1630, Milton had written *humming* tide, which is perhaps more expreffive and poetical. His firft epithet he had probably from the following fine paffage of Fletcher :

> While *humming* rivers by his cabin creeping,
> Rock foft his flumbering thoughts in quiet eafe.
>
> Eclog. 2.

Milton ufes *fyllable.* 208 Comus. Fletcher in his Mifcellanies, page 85, has *fyllabled.*

Milton is fomewhat indebted likewife to the Chrift's Victorie of Giles Fletcher. Our Lord is thus defcribed in the Wildernefs, by G. Fletcher :

> Seemed that man had them devoured all,
> Whome to devoure the beafts did make pretence,
> But him their falvage thirft did nought appall,
> Though weapons none he had for his defence :
> What armes for innocence, but innocence ?
> For when they faw their Lord's bright cognizance
> Shine in his face, foon did they difadvaunce,
> And fome unto him kneele, and fome about him daunce.

Downe

Downe fell the Lordly Lion's angrie mood,
And he himfelfe fell downe, in congies lowe;
Bidding him welcome to his waftfull wood,
Sometime he kift the graffe whear he did goe,
And, as to wafh his feete he well did knowe,
    With fauning tongue he lickt away the duft,
    And every one would neereft to him thruft,
And every one, with new, forgot his former luft.

Unmindfull of himfelfe, to minde his Lord,
The Lamb ftood gazing by the Tygers fide,
As though betweene them they had made accord,
And on the Lion's back the goate did ride,
Forgetfull of the roughnefs of the hide,
    If he ftood ftill, their eyes upon him bayted,
    If walk't, they all in order on him wayted,
And when he flept, they as his watch themfelves conceited.

After circumftantially defcribing the perfon of Jefus, Satan is thus introduced difguifed :

At length an Aged Syre farre off he fawe
Come flowely footing, everie ftep he gueft
One of his feete he from the grave did drawe,
Three legges he had, the woodden was the beft,
And all the way he went, he ever bleft
    With benedicities, and prayers ftore
    But the bad ground was bleffed ne'er the more,
And all his head with fnowe of age was waxen hore.

A good old Hermit he might feeme to be,
That for devotion had the world forfaken,
And now was travailing fome Saint to fee,
Since to his beads he had himfelfe betaken,
Whear all his former fin es he might awaken,
    And them might wafh a way with dropping brine,
    And almes, and fafts, and churches difcipline,
And dead, might reft his bones under the holy fhrine.

But when he neerer came, he lowted lowe
With prone obeyfance, and with curt'fie kinde,
That at his feete his head he feem'd to throwe ;
What needs him now another Saint to finde ?
&c. &c.

He

He thus exclaims with the moſt artful ſimplicity:

> Ah, mote my humble cell ſo bleſſed be
> As heav'n to welcome in his lowely roofe,
> And be the temple for thy deitie!
> Loe how my cottage worſhips thee aloofe,
> That under ground hath hid his head, in proofe
>   It doth adore thee with the feeling lowe,
>   Here honie, milke, and cheſnuts wild doe growe,
> The boughs a bed of leaves upon thee ſhall beſtowe.

Ch. Vict. 2 Can. Ed. 1610.

Compare Parad. Reg. 295. &c. Where our Saviour paſſed forty days in the wilderneſs:

> Nor taſted h man food, nor hunger felt
> Till thoſe days ended, hunger'd then at laſt
> Among wild beaſts: they at his ſight grew mild,
> Nor ſleeping him nor waking harm'd, his walk
> The fiery ſerpent fled, and noxious worm,
> The lion and fierce tiger glar'd aloof.
> But now an aged man in rural weeds
> Following, as ſeem'd 'the queſt of ſome ſtray ewe,
> Or wither'd ſticks to gather, which might ſerve
> Againſt a winter's day when winds blow keen,
> To warm him wet return'd from field at eve,
> He ſaw approach, who firſt w th curious eye
> Perus'd him, then with words thus utter'd ſpake.

MILTON.

How far the following Stanzas, which are but a continuation of what I before quoted, might have influenced Milton in his Comus, I leave the reader to determine. Fletcher is deſcribing the Bower of Vaine-Delight, to which our Lord is conducted by Satan:

> And all about, embayed in ſoft ſleepe,
> A heard of charmed beaſts aground were ſpread,
> Which the fair Witch in goulden chaines did keepe,
> And them in willing bondage fettered,
> Once men they liv'd, but now the men were dead,
>   And turn'd to beaſts, ſo fabled Homer old,
>   That Circe with her potion, charm'd in gold,
> Us'd manly ſoules in beaſtly bodies to immould.

Through

Through this falfe Eden, to his Leman's bowre,
(Whome thoufand foules devoutly idolize)
Our firft deftroyer led our Saviour.
Thear in the lower roome, in folemne wife,
They daunc't around, and powr'd their facrifice
    To plumpe Lyæus, and among the reft,
    The jolly prieft in yvie garlands dreft,
Chaunted wild Orgialls, in honour of the feaft.

Others within their arbours fwilling fat,
(For all the roome about was arboured)
With laughing Bacchus, that was growne fo fat,
That ftand he could not, but was carried,
And every evening frefhly watered,
    To quench his fierie cheeks, and all about
    Small cocks broke through the wall, and fallied out
Flaggons of wine, to fet on fire that fpueing rout.

This their inhumed foules efteem'd their wealths
To crowne the bouzing kan from day to night,
And ficke to drinke themfelves with drinking healths,
Some vomiting, all drunken with delight.
Hence to a loft, carv'd all in yvorie white,
    They came, whear whiter Ladies naked went,
    Melted in pleafure, and foft languifhment,
And funke in beds of rofes, amourous glaunces fent.

               Stan. 49, 50, 51, 52.

    After a defcription of Avarice and Ambition, we are prefented with the throne of *Panglo y,* who is thus defcribed :

A filver wande the Sorcereff. did fway,
And, for a crowne of gold, her haire fhe wore,
Onely a garland of rofe-buds did play
About her locks, and in her hand, the bore
A hollow globe of glaffe, that long before,
    She full of emptineffe had bladdered,
    And all the world therein depictured,
Whofe colours, like the rainbowe, ever vanifhed.

Thus the fpirit in Milton in giving directions to the brother, fpeaking of the Hæmony which he gives him as an antidote to the charms of Comus, fays :

——————— if you have this about you,
(As I will give you when we go) you may
Boldly affault the necromancers hall;
Where if he be, with dauntlefs hardihood,
And brandifh'd blade rufh on him, *break his glafs,*
And fhed the lufcious liquor on the ground,
But feize his wand.   647.

                            The

The Goddefs in Fletcher fings a fong of allurement, the fubject of which is Love (to ufe Milton's words), " Obtruding falfe rules prankt in reafon's garb," and endeavours to captivate our Saviour in the fame manner as Comus does the Lady, fee his fpeech at length, p. 706. A part of Fletcher's fong I produce for its elegance:

> See, fee the flowers that belowe,
> Now as frefh as morning blowe,
> And of all, the virgin rofe,
> That as bright Aurora fhowes,
> How they all unleaved die,
> Loofing their virginitie:
> Like unto a fummer-fhade,
> But now borne, and now they fade.
> Every thing doth paffe away,
> Thear is danger in delay,
> Come, come gather then the rofe,
> Gather it, or it you lofe.
> All the fande of Tagus fhore
> Into my bofome cafts his ore;
> All the va leys fwimming corne
> To my houfe is yeerely borne;
> Every grape of every vine
> Is gladly bruis'd to make me wine,
> While ten thoufand kings, as proud,
> To carrry up my traine, have bow'd,
> And a world of Ladies fend me
> In my chambers to attend me:
> All the ftarres in heav'n that fhine,
> And ten thoufand more, are mine;
>   Onely bend thy knee to me
>   Thy wooing fhall thy winning bee.

The effect of the fong on our Saviour is as follows:

> Thus fought the dire Enchauntrefs in his minde
> Her guilefull bayt to have embofomed,
>   But he her charmes difperfed into winde,
> And her of infolence admonifhed,
> *And all her optique glaffes fhattered.*

Milton ufes the very expreffion *fhatter'd.* 799 Comus.

I will conclude thefe obfervations on the two Fletchers with an extract from Howell's Letters. See Let. LXVI. *To E. Benlowes, Efq; upon the receipt of a Table of exquifit Latin Poems.* " I much thank you for your vifits, and other fair refpects you fhew me; efpecially that you have enlarged my quarters among thefe melancholy * walls, by fending me a whole Ifle to

---

* He was then confined in the Fleet.

walk

walk in, I mean that delicate *Purple Ifland* I received from you, wher I meet with *Apollo* and all his daughters, with other excellent fociety; I ftumble alfo ther often upon myfelf, and grow better acquainted with what I have within me, and without mee: infomuch that you could not make choice of a fitter ground for a prifoner, as I am, to pafs over than of that *Purple Ifle*, that *Ifle of Man* you fent me, which as the ingenious Author hath made it, is a far more dainty foil than that *Scarlet* ifland which lys near the *Baltic* fea." Edit. 1650. It is perhaps being triflingly minute to remark that Milton's " Sable *Stole* of Cyprus *lawn*." Il Pen. 35. might have originated from G. Fletcher.

> After them flewe the Prophets, brightly *ftol'd*
> In fhining *lawne*, and wimpled manifold.   Chr. Trium.

M. D R A Y T O N.

If we clofely confider the two following paffages from this poet, there will be no occafion to fuppofe with Dr. Farmer, (fee his Effay on the Learning of Shakefpear, p. 30.) that Milton in his juftly admired defcription of the Swan, had a paffage of Donne in his eye:

> ————————— the Swan with *arched neck*
> Between her white wings * mantling, *proudly rows*
> *Her ftate with oary feet.*   MILTON.

> The jealous Swan, there *fwimming in bis pride*
> With his *arch'd breaft* the waters did divide,
> His *faily wings* him forward ftrongly pufhing
> Againft the billowes with fuch furie rufhing,
> As from the fame, a fome fo white arofe
> As feem'd to mocke the breft that them oppofe.
> > Man in the Moone. p. 480. 1619 Edit.

---

* This word which is highly defcriptive, is applied by Spenfer to the Hawk:

> Ne is there hauke which *mantleth* her on perch.
> > 6 B. 11. C 32. F. Queen.

The

The Swan by his great mafter taught this good,
T' avoid the fury of the falling flood,
His *boat-like breaft, his wings rais'd for his fail,*
And *oar-like feet* ——   FLOOD.

Peck quotes an appofite paffage from Shakfpeare's Tempeft, from which
he fuppofes Milton to have taken his epithet *oary.* The lines are thefe :

> —————— his bold head
> 'Bove the contentious waves he kept, and *oard*
> Himfelf with his good arms in lufty ftrokes
> To th' fhore ——

But had Peck been a minute reader of Drayton, he would have found that
from him Milton copied the moft material features in his image. It is worthy of obfervation, that the idea of the Swan's having a mufical voice pre-
vails in Ireland, as well as in the writings of the Ancients. See Uno Von
Troil, fpeaking of this Bird. " They are faid to fing very harmonioufly in
the dark cold winters nights : but though it was in the month of September,
when I was upon the ifland, I never once enjoyed the pleafure of a fingle
fong." Letters on Iceland, p. 143.

The word *imparadis'd,* ufed by Milton, P. Loft. B. 4. p. 506. and fuppofed by fome of his firft commentators to have been coined by him, occurs twice in Drayton, perhaps oftener :

> Within the caftle hath the Queen devis'd
> A chamber with choice rarities fo fraught,
> As in the fame fhe had *imparadiz'd*
> Almoft what man by induftry hath fought.
>   Bar. Wars, B. 6. Stan. 30.

See alfo his Poly-Olbion :

> O my bright lovely brook whofe name doth bear the found
> Of God's firft garden-plot th' *imparadifed* ground
> Wherein he placed man.

The word feems to have been not uncommon with other of our older
Poets, as the following inftances prove :

> For fhe that can my heart *imparadife.*
>   Daniel. 12 Son.

> —————————— this *paradized* Earth.
>   Warner's Alb Eng 10 B. 60 Ch. Edit. 1602.

> Thou fitt'ft *emparadis'd,* and chaunt'ft eternall layes.
>   P. Fletcher's P. Ifl. C 1. St. 14. Edit. 1633.

As in his burning throne he fits *emparadis'd.*
> G. Fletcher's Chrift's Triumph.
> Stan. 43. Part. 2. Ed. 1610.

My foule's *imparadis'd* for 'tis with her.
> Habington's Caftara. Edit. 1640. p. 31.

Pope in the courfe of his Tranflation of Homer, in a variety of inftances, has with great happinefs and fuccefs availed himfelf of the opportunity of interweaving with his verfion applicable paffages from our beft poets, as Shakfpeare and Milton; perhaps in rendering the following line he had Milton in his eye:

'Ηέ π.θι κλολίμοιο μάσα σίάμα πιυκιλαγοϊ.   Il. 10. line 8.

Or bids the *brazen throat* of war to *roar.*   POPE.

But what he has here gained in ftrength, he has loft in accuracy. Homer fays nothing about *brazen*, Milton tempted him to ufe this epithet:

The *brazen throat* of war had ceas'd to *roar.*
> P. L. B. 11. p. 713.

I was induced to quote thefe paffages, as they will tend to introduce one of the moft nervous and fublime lines in the whole compafs of Engüfh Poetry. It is in our Author's Epiftle from Mortimer to Ifabel:

For which Rome fends her curfes out from far
Through the ftern throat of terror-breathing War.

S. DANIEL.

——————— my Silvia's memory
Is all that I muft ever live withal.   Scen. 4. Hym. Triumph.

This fimple thought reminds us of a moft inimitable exclamation in Shenftone's Epitaph on his amiable relation Mifs Doleman, who died of the fmall-pox at the age of 21. This little piece of Shenftone's is one of the very rare modern productions, that not only refembles but rivals the dignified and affecting concifenefs of the Ancients, in their fepulchral infcriptions. It is worth volumes of his paftorals. I will gratify myfelf by quoting it intire:

> Peramabili fuæ confobrinæ
> M. D.

                                        On

On the other fide.

Ah Maria
Puellarum elegantiffima,
Ah flore venuftatis abrepta,
Vale !
Heu quanto minus eft
cum reliquis verfari,
Quam tui
Meminiffe !

In our Author's funeral Poem to the memory of the Earl of Devonfhire,
the following lines remind us of the Immortal Chatham :

Here is no room to tell with what ftrange fpeed
And fecrefy he ufed to prevent
The enemies defigns : nor with what heed
He march'd before report : where what he meant
Fame never knew herfelf, till it was done.

Sylvefter, in his Du Bartas, compliments Daniel, and calls him

" My deer fweet Daniel, fharp-conceipted, brief,
Civill, fententious, for pure accents chief."   Fol. Edit. p. 82.

In what follows Drayton is alluded to, whom he intitles, " *our new Nafo.*"
Daniel had prefixed a Sonnet to his work.   B. Jonfon likewife has verfes
prefixed to it.

W.   B R O W N E.

There is an unftudied flow of mufic in many lines of this writer, that
perhaps exceeds almoft every thing of his contemporaries.   The harmony
of thefe lines are remarkable :

Fair was the day, but fayrer was the maide
Who that day's morne into the green woods ftraid.
Sweet was the aire but fweeter was her breathing,
Such rare perfumes the rofes are bequeathing.   B. 2. Song. 3.

Every poetical ear will be ftruck with the refemblance to Collins's :

Sad was the hour, and lucklefs was the day, &c.   2 Eclog.

The

The "ſimplex munditiis" of Horace is well imitated in the following expreſſion:

> ————————— underneath whoſe ſhade
> Moſt *neate in rudeneſſe* Nature arbors made.   4 Song. 1 B.

The thought in the concluding line of Pope's Epitaph on Gay, has (though
I cannot ſay I ſee any reaſon for it,) been in general diſapproved of by pro-
feſſed critics:

> But that the worthy and the good ſhall ſay,
> Striking their penſive boſoms—*here lies Gay.*

Browne has a ſimilar thought:

> No grave befits him but the hearts of men.   Vol. 1. p. 143.

But the thought is by no means uncommon; a variety of ſimilar paſſages might
be adduced. The laſt line but one of the Epitaph is more juſtly liable to
objection. I ſhould be glad to be informed of the difference between " the
" worthy and the good;" it is ſtrange, that Johnſon in his Criticiſm on this
Epitaph, ſhould have omitted to obſerve, that the ſecond line of it is borrowed from Dryden:

> Her wit was more than man, her innocence a child.
>   To the Mem. of Mrs. Killigrew.

In Browne's Paſtorals, B. 1. Song 5, there occurs a whimſical and ridiculous play upon words, in which Echo repeats the two laſt ſyllables of the
foregoing line which form an anſwer to it; the ſame thing occurs in Herbert's Temple, p. 182. Ed. 1709. See alſo Eraſmus's Colloquies. Butler
has treated this affectation with his uſual humour.

BISHOP HENRY KING.

Of whom Howell in his Letters, Vol. 2. p. 28. Edit. 1650. gives his opinion as follows: " You have much ſtreightened that knot of love, which
hath been long tied between us, by thoſe choice manuſcripts you ſent me
lately, amongſt which I find divers rare pieces, but that which afforded me
moſt entertainment in thoſe miſcellanies, was Dr. Henry King's Poems,
wherein I find not only heat and ſtrength, but alſo an exact concinnity and
evenneſs of fancy: they are a choice race of brothers, and it ſeems the ſame
genius diffuſeth itſelf alſo among the ſiſters:" I will quote alſo what follows, as it alludes to a ſiſter of our Author's. " It was my hap to be lately
where miſtreſs A. K. was, and having a paper of verſes in her hand, I got
it from her, they were an epitaph and an anagram of her own compoſure
and writing, which took me ſo far, that the next morning before I was up,
my rambling fancy fell upon theſe lines:

> *For the admitting of Miſtris* Anne King *to be the tenth Muſe.*

The

The verſes are not worth quoting. Dr. King, p. 88. of his Poems has verſes upon Mrs. Kirk's being unfortunately drowned in the Thames. There are ſome lines on the ſame ſubjeſt in " Elegies by Robert Heath, Eſq;" Lond. 1650. p. 1. In the Colleſtion of Dr. King's Poems, are the verſes On the Earl of Dorſet's death, which I have printed, p. 42. 2. Vol. They are to be found amongſt Biſhop Corbet's Poems, but to which of the two they belong I know not.

F I N I S.

(By *the* EDITOR *of theſe Volumes,*)

POEMS and other PIECES.

L O N D O N:

Printed for J. ROBSON, New-Bond Street.

MDCCLXXXVI.